This book is
Sara Craven (Annie Ashurst),
whose talent, humour and sharp wit are much missed.
And if you want a masterclass in writing romance
read *Comparative Strangers* (and prepare to tingle…).

THE GREEK'S BOUGHT BRIDE

SHARON KENDRICK

MILLS & BOON

First Published in Great Britain 2018
by Mills & Boon, an imprint of HarperCollins*Publishers*
1 London Bridge Street, London, SE1 9GF

© 2018 Sharon Kendrick

ISBN: 978-0-263-93464-9

This book is produced from independently certified FSC™ paper
to ensure responsible forest management.
For more information visit www.harpercollins.co.uk/green.

Printed and bound in Spain
by CPI, Barcelona

CHAPTER ONE

HE RECOGNISED HER straight away, though it took him a moment to remember why. Xan Constantinides gazed at the tiny redhead whose thick curls were tumbling over her shoulders and a flicker of something between desire and anger whispered across his skin. But he welcomed the distraction—however temporary—which allowed him to forget the promise he had made so long ago. Was it the wedding of one of his oldest friends which had pushed the unavoidable into prominence, or just the march of time itself? Because it was easy to believe that nothing would change. You acted as if the fast days weren't spinning into years. And then suddenly there it was—the future—and with it all those expectations...

A marriage he had agreed to.

A destiny he had always been determined to honour.

But there was no point in thinking about it now, not with a packed weekend lying ahead of him. Friendship and a valuable business partnership dictated he must attend the wedding of his friend the Sheikh, even though he usually avoided such events like the plague.

Xan returned his attention to the redhead. She was sitting on her own in the small terminal of the private airfield, waiting to board the luxury flight, the fiery disarray of her hair marking her out from the other women. Her clothes marked her out too and not simply because they were a far cry from the skimpy little cocktail dress she'd been wearing last time he'd seen her—an outfit which had sent his imagination soaring into overdrive, as it had obviously been intended to do.

Xan slanted her an assessing glance. Today there was no tight black satin Basque or skyscraper heels, nor fishnet stockings which had encased the most delicious pair of legs he had ever seen. No. She had taken the word *casual* and elevated it to a whole new level. Along with a pair of tennis shoes, she was wearing cut-off jeans which displayed her pale, freckled ankles and a plain green T-shirt which echoed the cat-like magnificence of her emerald eyes.

It was the eyes he remembered most. And the slender figure which had failed to fill out the curved dimensions of her skimpy uniform, unlike her over-endowed waitress colleagues who had been bursting out of theirs. And the way she had spilt the Old-Fashioned cocktail all over the table as she bent to serve him. The dripping concoction had caught his trouser leg—icy liquid spreading slowly over his thigh. He remembered flinching and the woman he'd been with snatching up her napkin to blot at it with attentive concern, even though he'd been in the middle of telling her that their relationship was over.

Xan's lips flattened. The redheaded waitress had straightened up and mouthed an apology but the defiant glint in her green eyes had suggested the sentiment wasn't genuine. For a moment he had found himself wondering if it had been a gesture of deliberate clumsiness on her part—but surely nobody would be that stupid?

Would they?

And now here she was in the most unexpected of places—waiting to board a luxury flight to the wedding of Sheikh Kulal Al Diya to the unknown Englishwoman, Hannah Wilson. Idly, Xan switched his cellphone to airplane mode as the redhead began to scrabble around inside an oversized bag which looked as if it had seen better days. Was she also a guest at the glittering royal marriage? His lips curved with something like contempt. Hardly. She was much more likely to have been hired to work at what was being described as the most glitzy wedding the desert region had seen for a decade. And in a country which demanded the most modest of dress codes, it was unlikely that she would be showing as much of her body as last time.

Pity.

Sliding the phone into his pocket, he allowed himself the faintest smile as she glanced up to notice him staring at her and a spark of something powerful passed between them. A full-blooded spark of sexual desire which fizzled almost tangibly in the air. Her magnificent eyes widened with disbelief. He saw the automatic thrust of her nipples against the thin T-shirt and his groin tightened in response.

Sometimes, Xan thought, with a frisson of anticipation, sometimes fate handed you something you hadn't even realised you wanted.

It was him.

It was definitely him.

What were the *chances*?

Somehow Tamsyn managed to stop her jaw from dropping—but only just. She'd been expecting the great and the good to be gathered together here at this small airport, ready to board the royal flight which would whisk them to Zahristan, but she hadn't really been paying attention to the other guests as they were all being guided into the small departure lounge. She'd only just got her head around the incredible fact that her sister Hannah was about to marry a desert king and would soon become a real-life queen. And even though Hannah was pregnant with the Sheikh's baby and such an unlikely union made sense on so many levels, Tamsyn hadn't quite managed to contain her disgust at the proposed nuptials. Because in her opinion, the man her sister was marrying was arrogant and domineering—and it seemed he chose his friends on the same basis.

She stole another sneaky look at the Greek billionaire who was lolling against a sofa on the other side of the small terminal, his exquisitely cut suit doing nothing to disguise the magnificence of his muscular body. Xan Constantinides. An unforgettable name for an unforgettable man. But would he remember her?

Tamsyn offered up a silent prayer. *Please don't let him remember her.*

After all, it was months and months ago and only the briefest of encounters. She bit the inside of her lip. Oh, *why* had she decided to send out a message of sisterly solitude to the woman the tycoon had been in the process of dumping in the swish bar where she'd been working? At least until her employment had come to a swift but wholly predictable termination...

She'd noticed Xan Constantinides from the moment

he'd walked into the twinkly cocktail bar. To be fair, everyone had noticed him—he was that kind of man. Charismatic and radiating power, he seemed oblivious to the stir of interest his appearance had created. Ellie, one of the other waitresses and Tamsyn's best friend, had confided that he was a mega-rich property tycoon who had recently been voted Greece's most eligible bachelor.

But Tamsyn hadn't really been listening to the breathless account of his bank balance or his record of bedding beautiful women before callously disposing of them. His physical presence made his wealth seem almost insignificant and she surprised herself by staring at him for longer than was strictly professional, because she wasn't usually the sort of cocktail waitress who ogled the better-looking male customers. And there had never been a customer quite as good looking as *this* one. She remembered blinking as she registered a physique which suggested he could easily go several rounds in the boxing ring and emerge looking as if he'd done nothing more strenuous than get out of bed. When you teamed a body like that with sinfully dark hair, dark-fringed eyes the colour of cobalt and a pair of lips which were both sensual and cruel—you ended up with a man who exuded a particular type of danger. And Tamsyn had always been very sensitive to danger. It was a quality which had hovered in the background during her troubled childhood like an invisible cosh—just waiting to bang you over the head if you weren't careful. Which was why she avoided it like the plague.

She remembered feeling slightly wobbly on her high-heeled shoes as she'd walked over to where the

Greek tycoon had been sitting with the most beautiful blonde Tamsyn had ever seen, when she heard the woman give an unmistakable sniff.

'*Please*, Xan,' she was saying softly, her voice trembling. 'Don't do this. You must know how much I love you.'

'But I don't *do* love. I told you that right from the start,' he'd drawled unequivocally. 'I explained what my terms were. I said I wouldn't change my mind and I haven't. Why do women refuse to accept what is staring them in the face?'

Tamsyn found the interchange infuriating. *Terms*? He was talking as if he was discussing some kind of business deal, rather than a relationship—as if his lovely companion was an object rather than a person. All she could think was that a woman didn't just come out and tell a man they loved them, not without a certain degree of encouragement. Her irritation had intensified while she'd waited for the barman to mix two Old-fashioned cocktails and when she'd returned she had noticed Xan Constantinides watching her. She wasn't sure which had annoyed her more—the fact that he was regarding her with the lazy assessment of someone who'd just been shown a shiny car and was deciding whether or not he'd like to give it a spin—or the fact that her body had responded to that arrogant scrutiny in ways which she didn't like.

She remembered the peculiar melting sensation low in her belly and the distracting tingle of her breasts pushing against the too-skimpy top of her uniform. She remembered being acutely aware of those cobalt eyes being trained on her, uncaring of the woman beside him who was trying very hard not to cry. And

Tamsyn had felt a kick of anger. Men. They were all the same. They took and they took and they never gave back—not unless they were forced into a corner. Even then they usually found some way of getting out of it. No wonder she deliberately kept them at arm's length. With an encouraging smile she'd handed the woman her drink, but as she lifted the Greek's cocktail from the tray, Tamsyn had met a gaze full of sensual mockery.

She told herself afterwards that she hadn't deliberately angled the glass so that it sloshed all over the table and started to seep onto one taut thigh, but she couldn't deny her satisfaction when he recoiled slightly, before the blonde leapt into action with her napkin.

She was sacked soon afterwards. The bar manager told her it was a culmination of things, and spilling a drink over one of their most valued customers had been the final straw. Apparently she wasn't suited to work which required a level of sustained calm, and she reacted in a way which was inappropriate. Secretly she'd wondered whether Xan Constantinides had got her fired. Whether he was yet another powerful man throwing his weight around and getting the world to jump when he ordered it to. Just like she wondered if he would remember her now.

Please don't let him remember her now.

'Would all passengers please begin boarding? The royal aircraft will be departing for Zahristan in approximately thirty minutes.'

Obeying the honeyed instruction sounding over the Tannoy, Tamsyn bent to pick up her rucksack as she rose to her feet. Didn't matter if he remembered her because he was nothing to her. She was on this trip for one reason and that was to support Hannah on her wedding day, no matter how big her misgivings about her choice of groom. Because, despite having tried to persuade her big sister not to go through with such a fundamentally unsuitable marriage—her words had fallen on deaf ears. Either Hannah hadn't wanted to listen, or she hadn't dared—probably because she was carrying the desert King's baby and there was all that stuff about him needing a legitimate heir. Tamsyn sighed as she rose to her feet. She had done everything she could to influence her sister but now she must accept the inevitable. She would pick up the pieces if necessary and be there for her—just as Hannah had always been there for her.

Hooking her bag over her shoulder, she trooped behind the other passengers—many of whom seemed to know each other—thinking this was like no journey she'd ever been on, with none of that pre-flight tension which usually made everyone so uptight. But then she'd always flown budget before—with that feeling of being herded onto the aircraft like wildebeest on the Serengeti, followed by a futile attempt to claim a few inches of space in the overhead locker. Not so on this flight. The glossy attendants looked like models and were unfailingly polite to all the passengers, as they gestured them forward.

And suddenly Tamsyn heard the sound of a deeply accented voice behind her. Rich and resonant, it sounded like grit being stirred into a bowlful of molasses. She felt her throat dry. She'd heard it once when it had cursed aloud in Greek before asking her what the hell she was playing at. It had made her spine tingle then and it was making it tingle now as the powerful Greek tycoon moved to stand beside her.

Tamsyn stared up into a pair of cold blue eyes and wished her heart would stop crashing against her ribcage. Just like she wished her nipples would cease from hardening so conspicuously against her cheap T-shirt. But her senses were refusing to obey her as Xan Constantinides dominated her field of vision, his presence imprinting itself on her consciousness in a way she could have done without.

She noticed how softly his olive skin gleamed beneath the pristine cuffs of his snowy shirt. And that he carried with him a faint scent of sandalwood, underpinned with the much more potent scent of raw masculinity. Somehow he seemed to suck in all the available oxygen around them, leaving her feeling distinctly short of breath. He was the epitome of vibrancy and life, and yet there was a darkness about him too. Something unsettling and strangely *perceptive* in the depths of those amazing cobalt eyes. Suddenly Tamsyn felt vulnerable as she looked up at him and that scared her. Because she didn't do vulnerability. Just like she didn't react to men—especially men like this. It was her trademark. Her USP. Beneath her fiery exterior beat a heart of pure ice, and that was the way she intended to stay.

She told herself not to panic. People were slowly filing forward and in a few minutes she'd be safely on the plane and hopefully sitting as far away from him as possible. If it had been a commercial flight she would have been perfectly entitled to ignore him, but this was not a commercial flight. They were all guests at the same exclusive royal wedding and even

Tamsyn's shaky grasp on protocol warned her that she mustn't be rude.

But she could certainly be cool. She didn't have to gush or be super-friendly. She didn't owe him anything. She was no longer in the subservient role of waitress and could say exactly what she wanted.

'Well, well, well,' he murmured, his English faultless as he pulled his passport from the inside pocket of his suit jacket. 'Fancy seeing you here.'

Tamsyn fixed her face into a mildly questioning expression. 'I'm sorry? Have we met?'

Cobalt eyes narrowed. 'Well, unless you have a doppelganger,' he drawled. 'You're the waitress who hurled a drink into my lap last summer. Surely you can't have forgotten?'

For a moment Tamsyn was tempted to tell him that yes, she had forgotten. She thought about pretending she'd never seen him before, but suspected he would see through her. Because nobody would ever forget crossing paths with a man like Xan Constantinides, would they? Not unless they were devoid of all their senses. She gave him a steady look. 'No,' she said. 'I haven't forgotten.'

His eyes narrowed. 'I was thinking about it afterwards and wondering if you made a habit of throwing drinks all over your customers.'

She shook her head. 'Actually, no. It's never happened before.'

'Just with me?'

'Just with you,' she agreed.

There was a pause. 'So was it deliberate?'

She considered his silky question and answered it as honestly as she could. 'I don't think so.'

'You don't *think* so?' he exploded. 'What kind of an answer is that?'

She heard his incredulity and as Tamsyn met his piercing gaze she suddenly wanted him to know. Because maybe nobody had ever told him before. Maybe nobody had ever pointed out that the opposite sex were not something you could just dispose of, as if you were throwing an unwanted item of clothing into the recycling bin. 'I'm not going to deny that I felt sorry for the woman you were dumping.'

He frowned, as if he couldn't work out which particular woman she was talking about. As if he were running over a whole host of candidates who might have fitted the bill. And then his face cleared. 'Ah, *neh*,' he murmured in his native tongue, before the frown reappeared. 'What do you mean, you felt sorry for her?'

Tamsyn shrugged. 'She was clearly very upset. Anyone could see that. I thought you could have done it in a kinder way. Somewhere more private, perhaps.'

He gave a short and disbelievingly laugh. 'You're saying you made a negative judgement of me based on a few overheard words of conversation?'

'I know what I saw,' said Tamsyn doggedly. 'She seemed very upset.'

'She was.' His eyes narrowed. 'Our relationship was over but she refused to believe it, and this time she needed to believe it. We hadn't seen each other for weeks when she asked to meet me for a drink and I agreed. And I left her in no doubt that I couldn't give her what she wanted.'

Slowly Tamsyn digested all this, her curiosity aroused in spite of herself. 'What was it she wanted that you were unable to give her?'

He smiled at her then—a brief, glittering smile which momentarily made one of the female ground staff turn and look at him in dazed adoration.

'Why marriage, of course,' he said softly. 'I'm afraid it's an inevitable side-effect of dating women—they always seem to want to push things on to the next level.'

It was several seconds before Tamsyn could bring herself to answer. 'Wow,' she breathed. 'That is the most arrogant thing I've ever heard.'

'It may be arrogant, but it's true.'

'Has nobody ever dumped *you*?'

'Nobody,' he echoed sardonically. 'How about you?'

Tamsyn wondered why she was having a conversation like this while waiting in line to get on a plane but, having started it, it would be pathetic to call time on it just because he'd touched on a subject she found difficult. No, she had never been dumped, but then she'd only ever had one relationship which she'd ended as soon as she realised that her body was as frozen as her heart. But she wasn't going to tell Xan Constantinides that. She didn't have to tell him anything, she reminded herself, replacing his question with one of her own.

'Did you complain about me to the management?'

He dragged his gaze away from the pert stewardess, who was ticking off passenger names on her clipboard. 'No. Why?'

'I got the sack soon after.'

'And you think I orchestrated it?'

She shrugged. 'Why not? It happened to my sister. The man she's marrying actually got her fired from her job.'

'Well, for your information, no—I didn't. I have

enough staff of my own to look after without keeping tabs on those employed by other people, no matter how incompetent they are.' There was a pause. 'What happened to your sister?'

It occurred to Tamsyn he didn't have a clue who she was. That he had no idea it was the Sheikh himself who'd got her sister fired, or that after Saturday's glittering ceremony he would be her new brother-in-law. To Xan Constantinides, she was just a judgmental cocktail waitress who couldn't hold a job down and he probably thought it ran in the family. 'Oh, you wouldn't know her,' she said truthfully, because Hannah had confided that she hadn't yet met any of her Sheikh fiancé's friends and was absolutely *terrified*, because they were all so high-powered.

Their conversation was halted by a smiling stewardess with a clipboard and as she was given her seat number, Tamsyn turned back to Xan Constantinides with a forced smile.

'Nice talking to you,' she said sarcastically and saw his navy eyes darken. 'Enjoy the flight.'

Her heart was still pounding as she took her seat on the aircraft and picked up the book she'd so been so looking forward to—a crime thriller set in the Australian outback—which she'd hope would pass away the hours during the long journey to Zahristan's capital city of Ashkhazar. But it was difficult to concentrate on the rather lurid plot, when all she could think about was the powerful Greek who'd managed to have such a potent effect on her. She tried to sleep, and failed. She stared out of the window at the passing clouds which looked like thick fields of cotton wool. She attempted to tuck into the variety of delicious foodstuffs which were placed before her, but her appetite seemed to have deserted her. She was just thinking gloomily about the days of celebration ahead of her, when that gravelled molasses voice broke into her thoughts.

'I suppose you'll be working as soon as we get there?'

Tamsyn looked up to see that Xan Constantinides had stopped in the aisle right beside her seat and was deigning to speak to her. She looked up to meet that distracting cobalt stare. 'Working?' she echoed in confusion.

'I'm assuming that's why you're here,' he murmured.

Suddenly Tamsyn understood. He thought she was here to act as a waitress at the royal wedding!

Well, why wouldn't he think that? She certainly wasn't dressed like the other women on the flight, with their discreet flashes of gold jewellery which probably cost a fortune and their studiedly casual designer outfits. Her sister had tried to insist on buying her some new clothes before the wedding, but Tamsyn had stubbornly refused. Because hadn't Hannah helped her out too many times in the past—and hadn't she vowed she was going to go it alone from now on?

'Just because you're going to marry a rich man, doesn't mean *I* have to accept his charity,' she remembered responding proudly. 'Thanks all the same, but I'll wear what's already in my wardrobe.'

Was that why Xan Constantinides was so certain she was a member of staff rather than a wedding guest? Because she was wearing old sneakers rather than those fancy shoes with the red soles which everyone else seemed to be sporting? Suddenly, Tamsyn thought she could have a bit of fun with this and liven up a wedding she was dreading. Wouldn't it be priceless to have the Greek tycoon patronise her—before he discovered her connection to the royal house of Al Diya?

She met his scrutiny with a bashful shrug. 'Yes,' she said. 'An event like this pays very well and they wanted to have some British serving staff among the Zahirstanians. You know, to make sure the English-speaking guests felt at home.'

He nodded. 'Good of them to fly you out in style.'

Tamsyn bit back an indignant laugh. Any minute now and he would start asking her if she'd ever been on an airplane before! She reached out and gave the plush leather of the armrest a quick squeeze, as if it was the chubby cheek of a particularly attractive little baby. 'I know,' she sighed. 'Let's hope I don't get too used to all this luxury before I go back to my poverty-stricken existence.'

'Let's hope not.' His smile was brief and dismissive—the smiling equivalent of a yawn—as if he had already grown bored with her. His gaze drifted towards the curvy bottom of one of the stewardesses, as if already he was miles away. 'And now, if you don't mind—I have work to do.'

Tamsyn opened her mouth to say that *he* was the one who had started the conversation, but something made her shut it again, as he continued his journey up the aisle of the plane. And she wasn't the only person looking at him—every female on the plane seemed to be following his sexy progress towards the front of the aircraft. Resentfully, Tamsyn found herself noting the powerful set of his shoulders and the way thick, dark tendrils of hair curled around the back of his neck.

She thought she'd never seen a man who was quite so sure of himself. He seemed to inject the air around him with a strange and potent energy and she resented the effect he seemed to have on her without even trying.

An unfamiliar shiver whispered its way down her spine and she clenched her hands into tense little fists as the plane soared through the sky on its way to the desert kingdom.

CHAPTER TWO

TAMSYN STOOD IN the centre of the huge room, her head
spinning as she gazed around her in amazement. She'd
known that her sister's fiancé owned an actual palace
which she was going to be staying for the forthcom-
ing wedding celebrations, but the reality of being here
was so far outside her experience that for a moment
she felt as if she were dreaming.

Drinking in her surroundings, she craned her neck
to look up at the high ceiling which was vaulted and
gilded with gold. She didn't think she'd ever seen so
much gold! Soft drapes fell from the floor-to-ceiling
windows which overlooked surprisingly green and
lush gardens—surprising, because this was, after all,
a desert country. Her bed was huge and closer to the
ground than she was used to and it was covered with
rich brocade and velvet cushions. And everywhere she
looked she could see flowers. Big, claret-coloured and
sunset-hued roses crammed into what looked like solid
gold vases. Their heavy scent vied with the incense
which was burning softly in one corner, in a container
which seemed to be studded with genuine rubies and
emeralds. As for the bathroom, Tamsyn swallowed.
The bathroom was something else—exceeding the

standards of every upmarket hotel she'd ever worked in—and she'd worked in quite a few. She spent several minutes running her fingertips over the fluffy bath-robe and eying up the gleaming glass bottles of bath oil and perfume, wondering if she'd be able to take some of them home with her.

She had sent away the servant who had hovered around after her arrival, because just the thought of *having* a servant had made her feel uncomfortable, since that felt like *her* natural role. She'd thought she would be alone until she was summoned to the pre-wedding dinner, but a knock at the door interrupted her reverie and Tamsyn went to answer it, her eyes narrow-ing as she stared at the woman who was standing there. She was wearing beautiful silk robes of sapphire blue, which flowed to the ground like a waterfall. Her shiny hair was covered in some gauzy veil of silver and the sparkling earrings which dangled from her earlobes echoed the aquamarine brilliance of her eyes. Tamsyn stood in shocked silence, realising that for a few sec-onds she hadn't recognised *her own sister!*

'Hannah,' she breathed. 'Is that really you?'

Hannah came in and closed the door behind her, before enveloping Tamsyn in a crushing bear hug. 'Of course it's me—who did you think it was?'

Tamsyn gave a mystified shake of her head. 'I can't believe it. You look so different. Like…like a real-life queen.'

A wry smile touched her sister's lips. 'Well, that's kind of appropriate, seeing as of Saturday that's ex-actly what I'm going to be.'

Tamsyn stilled. Was she imagining the strained quality in Hannah's voice or the faint shadows around her eyes? 'You don't have to go through with it, you know,' she said instantly, but her sister shook her head.

'I'm afraid I do. I can't back out of it now and I don't want to. I have to do this—for the sake of the baby.'

At the mention of the baby, Tamsyn's gaze swivelled to her sister's belly. She supposed that most people might not even have guessed Hannah was pregnant—she looked more like someone who'd just come back from holiday having been a bit too liberal with the hotel buffet. But she knew Hannah better than anyone. Hannah who had acted more like a mother than a big sister when they were growing up. They had shared a mother who had given them up when they'd been very young—but they each had different fathers.

Just the thought of *fathers* made an acrid taste rise up in Tamsyn's throat because her own had been a waster in every which way. She tried her best not to judge all men by his miserable standards, but sometimes it was difficult. But then, life was difficult, wasn't it? Everyone knew that. These days she understood why Hannah had kept her in the dark about her parentage for so long, though she had been bitter and angry about it for a long time. But now was not the time to rake up the perceived sins of the past. She was here, not because she wanted to be—but because she was determined to support her beloved sister—the only family she had left in the world.

'So what's it like living with a sheikh? Is Kulal treating you properly?' she demanded.

Hannah shot a nervous glance in the direction of the door as if she was afraid someone might be standing outside, listening.

'He is.' The Princess-in-waiting forced a smile. 'How was your flight?'

Tamsyn hesitated, thinking it would probably be unwise to offload onto her pregnant sister on the eve of her wedding. No need to mention that she'd met Xan Constantinides once before and certainly no need to mention that she'd tipped a drink over him. 'Very comfortable,' she said. She saw Hannah frown—as if she hadn't been expecting such polite diplomacy so she injected her next remark with just the right amount of carelessness. 'I bumped into some Greek tycoon in the queue.'

'Xan Constantinides?'

'That's him.' Tamsyn paused and then, despite her best intentions, she couldn't resist her next comment. 'He's pretty full of himself, isn't he?'

Hannah shrugged. 'Why wouldn't he be? He made billions at an early age and is built like a Greek god. Apparently women fall at his feet like ninepins and I guess those kind of things can go to a man's head. And of course, he's never been married—which makes him a bit of a target for predatory women. Never even got close, so Kulal tells me.' She frowned. 'You didn't... you didn't fall for him did you, Tamsyn?'

'Oh, please!' Tamsyn manufactured a disbelieving snort. 'I don't go for men with egos the size of Mars.'

'And you didn't fall *out* with him, I hope?' continued Hannah nervously.

'Oh, come on, Han. As if I could be bothered!' Tamsyn gave an airy shrug. 'Why, I barely exchanged two words with the man.'

'Good. Because Kulal is very fond of him and they're in the middle of some hugely important business deal together.' Hannah smoothed down her silky robes, the movement drawing attention to her massive diamond engagement ring which glittered on her finger like a constellation of stars. 'But that's enough about Xan. I thought we could discuss your wardrobe.'

'My wardrobe?' Tamsyn's eyes narrowed with suspicion. 'What about it?'

There was a pause, during which Hannah seemed to be choosing her words with care. 'Tammy, what are you planning to wear to the rehearsal dinner tonight?'

Tamsyn had been waiting for this. Bad enough that Hannah seemed to have morphed into someone completely different—ever since the arrogant Sheikh had swept into her life and carried her off to his desert kingdom. Why, she barely recognised the elegant creature who stood before her as the same person who had once made beds for a living as a chambermaid at the Granchester Hotel. But that didn't mean *she* had to do the same, did it?

'I've got a very nice dress I bought down the market,' she said. 'I'm going to wear that. And how many times do I have to tell you not to call me Tammy?'

'Tamsyn, you *can't*. You can't wear some dress you've bought down the market to a royal wedding!'

'Why not?'

'Because…because….' Distractedly Hannah began to pace around the vast suite, her silken robes swishing against the floor as she moved. 'Well, the guest list is pretty daunting, if you want the truth. Even to me. Especially to me,' she added, on a whisper.

'I'm not daunted by other people's wealth,' said Tamsyn proudly.

'I know you're not—and there's no reason you should be. It's just…'

'Just what? Come on, Hannah—spit it out.'

Hannah drew to a halt beside Tamsyn's open suitcase, shooting a quick glance inside before sucking in a big breath which failed to hide her instinctive grimace. 'You can't wear any old thing,' she said gently, as she turned to look at her sister. 'Not to a function as important as this. It's my wedding and you're my sister. I'm the bride and the groom just happens to be a desert king. People are going to be looking at you, you know—especially as you're the only family I've got.'

Tamsyn's first instinct was to say she didn't care what other people thought. And if she fancied wearing her canvas sneakers beneath the dress she'd picked up for a bargain price—then that's exactly what she would do. But something about Hannah's anxious face tugged at a conscience she would prefer not to have. Suddenly she recognised that any defiance in the clothes department might reflect badly, not necessarily on her—but on her sister. And hadn't Hannah always done so much for her? Cared for and protected her during those deprived days of their fractured childhood…didn't she owe her for that?

'I don't have any fancy clothes,' she mumbled, feeling once again like the little girl who'd been mocked in the school playground because there was nothing in her lunchbox but a few scraps of bread and jam. *You're poor*, the other children used to taunt—and Tamsyn had been too ashamed to admit that her foster father had spent all his money on gambling and womanising and her foster mother had been too weak to object. Her education had suffered as a consequence and she'd left school without qualifications, which didn't exactly make her a big player in the job stakes. Money remained tight for Tamsyn and what little money she *did* have she certainly wasn't going to waste on an expensive dress she'd only get to wear once. 'I'm not stupid, Hannah,' she said huffily. 'I'm not planning to let you down. I'll make the best of what I have, just like I've always done.'

'I know you will. And when you bother to pull out all the stops you can look amazing. But this is different. I don't want you and I to stick out any more than we already are. So let me give you something to wear, Tamsyn. Something beautiful—the like of which you will never have worn before.' There was a pause. 'Please.'

Tamsyn had vowed she wasn't going to accept any more of Hannah's charity, no matter how scared she was about the future. Her latest job in a café paid only peanuts and in the meantime her overdraft was getting steadily bigger. The latest blow had been the recent rent raise on her crummy little apartment, leaving her wondering how on earth she was going to pay it.

She thought about the glamourous women she had travelled over with on the Sheikh's private plane and wondered what glorious surprises they would be pulling out of their suitcases for the glittering dinner tonight. And then she thought about a pair of cobalt eyes and the way they had trained themselves on her. She'd seen the way the Greek's gaze had focussed in on her scruffy tennis shoes and the disdainful curve of his lips in response. Was it that which made her suddenly decide to take up her sister's offer? To dress up for the party so that she might fit in, for once in her life?

'Okay. You can find me something to wear, if you like,' she said, casting a doubtful glance at Hannah's covered head. 'But I'm definitely not wearing a veil.'

Peering into the silvered surface of the antique mirror, Xan gave his tie a final unwanted tug. Raking his fingers back through the raven disarray of his hair he did his best to stifle a yawn as he deliberated on how he was going to get through the long evening ahead.

He *hated* these affairs with a passion and part of him felt deeply sorry for his royal friend, for being forced to marry some gold-digging little chambermaid from England. Contemptuously, his lips curved into their habitual line of disapproval. How could Kulal— a desert king renowned for an extensive list of sophisticated lovers—have fallen for the oldest trick in the book? There had been no official announcement but you wouldn't need to be a mathematician to work out that a hasty wedding arranged between one of the region's most exalted sheikhs and an unknown commoner—was bound to end up with a baby a few months down the line. Had the chambermaid deliberately trapped him, he mused? And if so, how could his friend bear the thought of that deception for all those long years which lay ahead?

He thought of his own marital destiny and not for the first time, began to see that it could have much to commend it, because Sofia was sweet and undemanding. He couldn't imagine her ever trying to trap him by falling pregnant—probably because he doubted she would ever consent to sex before marriage. His mouth hardened for it was many months since he had seen his unofficial fiancée and he knew he couldn't keep putting it off their arranged marriage indefinitely. Up until now it had been a private and completely confidential agreement between two families, but the longer he stalled, the more likely that the press would get hold of it and have a field day with it. His jaw clenched. He would set in motion the formal courtship when he flew out of here after the weekend, with a wedding pencilled in for the middle of next year.

But for now he was still technically a free man and unwillingly his thoughts turned to lust, for it had been a while since he had enjoyed a woman in his bed.

He was discreet about his relationships—for obvious reasons—and nobody outside their immediate families knew he had been promised to a beautiful young Greek girl. His recent sexual abstinence had certainly not been caused by a lack of opportunity— but because he had become jaded and bored by the attentions of predatory women on the make.

He scowled at his reflection before turning away. The press didn't help his endeavours to maintain a low profile and he cursed the obsession which made certain newspapers speculate about when he intended to tie the knot. Wasn't it such careless speculation which caused women to pursue him, as if they were hunting down some particularly elusive quarry? Didn't they realise that the chase was the thing which fired up a man's blood? Xan's mouth flattened. At least, that was what he had been told—for he had never had to pursue a woman. They came after him in their droves, like dedicated ants flocking to a spoonful of spilled honey. Some he enjoyed and others he discarded—but he made it plain to each and every one that there was no point in wishing for any kind of future with him, though he never explained why. And wasn't the truth that he enjoyed the protective barriers which his long-term engagement placed around him? It kept women at a safe distance and that was the way he liked it.

A servant came to fetch him to take him to the pre-wedding dinner and Xan quickly became aware of the excitement in the air as the wedding grew closer. Tall, burning flames lit the courtyard and in the distance he could hear the low beat of unfamiliar music which only added to the febrile build of atmosphere. Through wide corridors scented with jasmine and gardenia and lit with gold and silver candles, he followed the silent servant—taking his place at last in some inordinately grand ballroom, which he hadn't seen on his last visit.

He had visited Zahristan once before, when Kulal had taken him out to the desert to see the state-of-the-art solar panels which the country's scientists had designed, and in whose manufacture Xan had invested a great deal of money. He had combined the work trip with some serious riding on the most magnificent stallion he'd ever mounted and then he and the Sheikh had camped beneath the blinding brilliance of the stars in an opulent Bedouin tent. Xan remembered thinking that his powerful royal friend had the world at his fingertips—yet now he was being forced into a corner, trapped into a relationship he did not really want.

And wasn't exactly the same thing happening to *him*? Briefly Xan thought about the Greek girl with dark eyes who was everything a man could possibly desire. No. He was walking into his future with his eyes open. Not for him the lottery of chance or ignorance. There would be no skeletons emerging from the closet of Sofia, for she was someone he had known all her life. She was pure and beautiful and… His mouth hardened as he allowed the unwanted thought to flit into his mind.

The chemistry would come later.

Most of the other guests were already assembled in the huge gilded ballroom, which led into a banqueting hall almost as vast. Beneath chandeliers which glittered like shoals of priceless diamonds, women paraded in their finery, the men beside them wearing dark suits, desert robes or uniform. For some reason Xan found himself looking round for the redheaded waitress but couldn't see her anywhere and he wondered if she was somewhere deep in the palace kitchens, loading up her tray. Instead, he accepted a drink from someone else—a sharp-sweet cocktail containing fire-berry juice and drank it silently as they awaited the arrival of the royal couple.

At last, a single musician stepped forward to play a fanfare on the traditional *mizmar*, heralding the arrival of the Sheikh and his bride-to-be and there was a murmur of expectation as the couple paused in the open doorway of the ballroom and all heads turned in their direction.

And then he saw her.

Xan's fingers tightened around his drink so tightly that for a moment he was afraid that the delicate glass might shatter. He expelled a long, low breath as his disbelieving gaze settled on the feisty redhead who was following behind the royal couple as if it was her every right to do so.

His eyes narrowed. No sawn-off jeans and canvas shoes tonight. She was wearing an exquisite dress of emerald silk which matched the brilliance of her eyes and looked as if had been made just for her. The design was simple and in many ways modest, but it accentuated her body in a way which her sexy cocktail waitress uniform had failed to do. In that rather *obvious* black satin ensemble she had looked more like a little girl playing dress-up, while tonight she looked like a woman. Xan swallowed. A very sensual woman. Her lustrous red curls had been caught back, displaying dazzling diamond and emerald earrings which brushed the sides of her long neck. He felt the pooling of blood at his groin and suddenly she turned her head to look directly at him—as if some sixth sense had told her he was staring. A faint flicker of triumph illuminated her extraordinary eyes before, very deliberately, she turned her back on him and began chatting to a tall man in some sort of military uniform who seemed to be devouring her with his hungry gaze.

Xan felt the hard beat of a pulse at his temple. He had imagined her gliding around between the guests with a tray of drinks in her hand and this sudden unexpected elevation of status left him feeling confused. If she wasn't a waitress, then who the hell *was* she? He found himself dipping his head to speak to the blonde woman beside him who had been slowly edging herself closer in a way which was boringly predictable.

'Who is that woman in green?' he questioned silkily. 'The one who entered with the Sheikh and his fiancée.'

The blonde gave a discernible pout of disappointment followed by a slight shrug. 'Her? Her name is Tamsyn,' she said reluctantly. 'Tamsyn Wilson. She's the sister of the bride.'

Xan nodded as suddenly it all made sense. The reason why she had been dressed down and out of place on the flight over. The reason why a cocktail waitress was hobnobbing with one of the most powerful royal families in the world. Wilson. Of course. The bride's sister. The bride who had trapped his friend into marriage by getting pregnant. Xan gave a short laugh. How the redhead must have been laughing to herself when he'd made the—very understandable—assumption that she was here on a working trip. Was she enjoying the fact that he'd made such a fundamental mistake? He watched as she walked straight past him, ignoring him completely, her glorious fiery head held high in the air. And he felt the corresponding roar of his blood in response.

It was a long time since Xan could remember the minutes passing so slowly and never had he been so comprehensively ignored by the person he most wanted to speak to. He'd never had to work to get a woman to join him—usually the briefest of glances would send them scuttling over with an eagerness which was sometimes enough to kill his desire stone-dead. But Tamsyn Wilson wasn't playing ball. He watched her dip her glorious red head to the side as the Sheikh introduced her to a group of people and he saw the automatic light of interest in the men's eyes. He thought about infiltrating the group and commandeering her for himself, but instinct told him such a plan would be foolish. Only a quick glance at the seating plan yielded up the satisfying information that once again, they were seated next to each other. Xan's lips curved into a smile of anticipation. Far better to have her captive at his side and then…

Then what?

He hadn't yet gone that far in his imagination, but the increased pound of blood at his groin gave him a very good idea of how he intended the evening to end. And why not? His formal courtship of Sofia had not yet started. Was it not better to indulge his desires and rid himself of them? To eradicate all restlessness before finally settling down?

The distinctive sound of the trumpet-like *mizmar* broke into the chatter as servants began guiding the guests towards the galleried dining room, where the gleam of the dazzling long table and the perfume of countless roses awaited them. Xan stood beside the vacant chair next to his, watching the redhead approach without any kind of smile on her face, the defiant spark of her eyes the only acknowledgement she had seen him.

In stony silence she came to stand beside him.

'So,' he said softly as the faint drift of her scent washed over his skin and it became clear she wasn't planning to greet him with any kind of rapturous joy. 'We meet again.'

Her expression was cool. 'It would seem so.'

'Would you care to sit down?'

She gave a sarcastic elevation of her eyebrows. 'Since the alternative is eating on the hoof, I suppose the answer must be yes.'

Her insolence was turning him on almost as much as the slender curve of her breasts beneath her exquisite green silk dress. Xan pulled out her chair, her mulish look indicating that such display of chivalry was unnecessary but as she lowered her bottom onto the carved golden seat his blood pressure rocketed once more. As he guided the chair back in, his fingers briefly brushed against her narrow shoulders and he had to resist the urge to let them rest there and to massage away the undeniable tension he could feel.

'You didn't tell me you were the bride's sister,' he said, as he sat down beside her.

'You didn't ask.' She turned to him, her eyes full of an emerald light which tonight seemed almost unworldly. 'You just *assumed* I was here to work, didn't you? To ferry drinks around and wait at table. That someone like me couldn't possibly be one of the guests.'

'Was that such a crazy assumption to make, given the circumstances?' he mused. 'Last time I saw you that's exactly what you were doing. You made no mention of your connection with the bride and you have to admit, you didn't exactly blend in with the other guests on the plane. At least,' he amended softly. 'Not until now.'

'Now that my sister has given me the dress she secretly had made for me?' she demanded hotly. 'Or forced me to wear a necklace I'm terrified is going to fall off and deplete the royal coffers by several million quid, is that what you mean?'

Xan found himself having to bite back a smile. 'You cannot deny that you look very different tonight.'

Tamsyn picked up a jewel-encrusted goblet and sipped at the cold fizzy water it contained. No, she wasn't going to deny she looked different but beneath her fine new trappings—she felt exactly the same. Like someone who never fitted in—not anywhere. And tonight the sensation of being out of place was even more acute than usual. It wasn't just that everyone here was richer than her and seemed happy in their own skins, her disorientation was compounded by the unfamiliar feelings which were ripping through her like a spring tide. Feelings which were hard to define and even harder to understand. She wondered why she was feeling such a powerful *desire* for the man beside her, even though he was the most arrogant person she'd ever met. She wondered why her skin had felt as if it were on fire when his fingertips had brushed against her shoulder blades. Or why, beneath this fancy dress which Hannah had foisted on her—the tips of her breasts were as raw as if someone had been rubbing them with sandpaper.

Remember how he looked down his nose at you when you were boarding the flight. Remember how upset that ravishing blonde had been when he'd been cold-heartedly dumping her in the cocktail bar.

Yet right now it was difficult to think about anything other than the smile which was softening the edges of his lips and making her wonder what it would be like to be kissed by Xan Constantinides. Her gaze twitched to his long olive fingers and once again her throat constricted with an unfamiliar surge of lust. Because she didn't *do* desire. It was yet another side of her character which made it hard for her to fit in. It was her own private and horrible little secret—or rather, it was *one* of them—that despite all the fiery promise of her looks, she was about as responsive as a piece of wood. Hadn't she been told that by men deeply unhappy that she wouldn't 'put out', until she'd stopped going out with men altogether because life was easier that way?

'No, I'm not going to deny I look different tonight,'

she said. 'Which is why I assume you're talking to me, which you clearly didn't want to do when you thought I was nothing but a lowly waitress. Or was it the sight of my canvas tennis shoes which made you decide I wasn't worthy of your time?'

He looked as if he was about to contest the point before seeming to change his mind and subjecting her to a smile of such intensity that Tamsyn's heart felt as if it was going to burst right out of her chest.

'Look, why don't we wipe the slate clean and start again?' he suggested smoothly, extending his hand with practised ease. 'I'm Xan Constantinides. Short for Alexandros, in case you were wondering.'

'I wasn't,' she said moodily.

And you're Tamsyn, aren't you?' he continued, undaunted. 'Tamsyn Wilson.'

Behind her unsmiling lips, Tamsyn gritted her teeth. He hadn't bothered finding out her name before, had he? But now he'd discovered she was related to Hannah, he was behaving *very* differently She glanced up at where the prospective bride and groom were sitting next to one another on some amazing dais. Hannah was smiling but Tamsyn knew her well enough to see the strain of the occasion on her face—*and* she was pregnant. And since Hannah had stressed that Xan was engaged in some important business with the Sheikh, then shouldn't she at least *try* to be polite to him, at least for the duration of the meal itself?

'Yes,' she said, as a delicate mango and walnut salad was placed in front of her. 'That's my name.'

'So why don't you tell me something about yourself, Tamsyn Wilson?'

Picking up a golden fork to half-heartedly push

her food around the plate, Tamsyn wondered what the Greek tycoon would say if she told him the truth. That if her parents had been married, her *real* surname would have been one of the most memorable in the world. But she had never used it. She'd never had the right to use it—not then and certainly not now. She looked into his cobalt eyes and tried to suppress the insane flutter of her heart. 'What would you like to know?'

He gave a shrug of his broad shoulders. 'Why don't we start with the obvious. You say you're no longer working at the Bluebird Club?'

'I told you—I was sacked.'

'So what are you doing instead?'

Perhaps if she hadn't been feeling so out of place then Tamsyn might have engaged in small-talk. She might have skated over her nomadic existence and pretended she was just like every other woman there. But somehow those words wouldn't come. Maybe Xan Constantinides was too unsettling a presence and those cobalt eyes too deeply penetrating. Because the idea of putting a positive spin on a life which had felt like it was spiralling out of control lately, suddenly seemed too big an ask. Why bother trying to impress someone who was only deigning to speak to her because she was soon to be related to the Sheikh?

'Oh, I have a terribly glamorous life—you wouldn't believe,' she said airily. 'I work in a coffee bar by day and stack supermarket shelves by night.'

He frowned. 'Those sound like very long hours.'

'Go straight to the top of the class, Mr Constantinides—they are.'

His eyes narrowed. 'Aren't you qualified to do anything other than waitress work?'

She put the golden fork back down on the plate with a clatter, her starter untasted. 'Actually, no, I'm not. Exams were never really my number one concern when I was at school.'

'So why not retrain to do something else?' he questioned as he lifted up his own goblet, his steady cobalt gaze surveying her over its jewelled rim. 'You seem bright enough.'

Tamsyn nearly laughed out loud and not just because the remark was deeply patronising. That was the trouble with rich people. They had no idea how the world really worked. They'd been cushioned by their wealth and privilege for so long, that they couldn't put themselves in someone else's shoes. 'And who's going to fund me while I do that?' she questioned, trying to keep her voice from shaking. 'When I've just had a rent raise from my landlord? And before you tell me to move to somewhere cheaper, I've lived in London all my life and can't imagine going anywhere else. Some problems don't have easy solutions, I'm afraid. Not unless you're prepared to throw wads of cash at them, which isn't an option for most people. Welcome to the real world, Mr Constantinides.'

Xan wondered if she was aware that her defiant words were causing her chest to heave, making it difficult for him not to stare openly at the silk-covered perfection of her breasts. With an effort he focussed his gaze on his wine glass, twirling the stem between his fingers and watching as the different jewels sparkled in the light from the overhead chandeliers. 'It's true I have made a sizeable amount of money,' he conceded. 'But that certainly doesn't guarantee a trouble-free life.'

'You mean like someone forgetting to peel your grapes for you, or your private jet failing to take off on time?'

'That's a rather predictable response, Tamsyn,' he mused softly. 'You know, I'm almost disappointed. I was hoping for something a little more original.'

'Oh, dear,' she said, pushing out her bottom lip in an exaggerated pout. 'The billionaire is disappointed. We can't have that, can we?'

He met the hectic glitter of her green gaze and the pooling at his groin increased. Xan shifted in his seat. He had tried to be polite but she was having none of it and he suspected he knew why. Because something was flowing between them. Something powerful. The kind of physical attraction he'd been encountering from women ever since he'd reached puberty though it had never felt like this before. Women didn't usually glare at him as if he was the devil incarnate, or try to rub him up the wrong way. He suspected that Tamsyn's supposed dislike of him was masking a much deeper response and that her darkened eyes were telling the real story. A flicker of a smile curved his lips. She wanted him just as much as he wanted her. And why not? Why not enjoy one final taste of freedom before destiny beckoned?

But he didn't intend spending the entire meal fighting with her and not simply because fighting was a bore. Because he understood the psychology of women only too well. They always wanted what they thought they couldn't have. She needed to understand that she was in danger of missing out if she continued to be insolent towards him. He would make her wait and make her squirm, so that by the time she came to him she would be so aroused that...

The pressure at his groin was almost unbearable as, very deliberately, he turned his back on her and began to speak to the Italian heiress to his right.

CHAPTER THREE

IT WAS JUST a wedding. That was all. Just a few more hours to get through before she could go home. That's what Tamsyn kept telling herself as she made her way towards the grand throne room, in yet another outfit which Hannah had insisted she wear. She supposed her sister must have secretly had all these clothes made for her before she arrived, but she couldn't deny that the long, floaty dress suited her. Unlike the dramatic emerald gown she'd worn to the rehearsal dinner last night, this one was a much gentler hue. The soft grey colour of a pigeon's wing, the bodice and silk-chiffon skirt were sprinkled with tiny crystals which sparkled like stars as she moved.

Tonight, the jewels she'd been loaned were diamonds—some more chandelier drop earrings, along with a priceless choker which blazed like ice fire around her neck. And just like last night, when Tamsyn glanced in the mirror before leaving her suite, she didn't recognise the image reflected back at her. To the outside world she looked sleek, expensive and polished but inside she felt....disgruntled. And although she hated the reason for her discontentment, she wasn't deluded enough to deny it. Because wasn't the truth that her irritation had been caused by Xan Constantinides ignoring her throughout most of the pre-wedding dinner? He'd been laughing and joking *in Italian* with that stunning woman on his other side and making out like *she* was invisible. And yes, she *had* been behaving in a particularly waspish manner beforehand, but even so...

She'd made her escape as soon as the food part of the evening was over. She'd gone back to her suite of rooms and run herself a deep and perfumed bath—then spent most of the night tossing and turning as the image of a man with black hair and cobalt eyes kept haunting her thoughts. More than once she'd awoken to find the tips of her breasts all pointy and aching and a molten heat throbbing between her thighs, causing her to writhe frustratedly between the fine cotton sheets. She'd told herself she needed to pull herself together and put the infuriating Greek right out of her mind, but somehow it wasn't turning out to be that easy.

The moment she entered the throne room, Xan Constantinides was the first person she saw, despite the fact that the Sheikh was already at the front of the gilded throne room, waiting for his bride. Tamsyn's heart gave a powerful lurch as she willed her face not to register any emotion.

He looked...

She swallowed against the sudden rawness in her throat. He looked delectable. In a charcoal suit which suited his colouring, he stood taller than any other man there else. Even more disturbing was the fact that he seemed to sense when she entered, because he turned his head and she was caught in that cobalt stare, making her feel as if she was imprisoned there. As if she *wanted* to be imprisoned there. She willed him not to come up and talk to her and then of course, she wished he would, but Tamsyn told herself to concentrate on the ceremony itself and to fix her eyes on the bride, who was just arriving.

Hannah looked gorgeous, her pregnancy bump a subtle swell and well disguised by her unusual wedding gown of beaten gold. She'd apologised for not making Tamsyn her bridesmaid, explaining that it wasn't Zahristanian custom to do so. Not that Tamsyn had minded. Marriage had always seemed such an outdated institution to her and one which rarely lasted. More than once she'd wondered why it couldn't be replaced by something more modern.

Yet she sensed the historical significance of the vows being made, though Hannah's voice was so low she could barely hear them and the Sheikh looked so stern that Tamsyn was certain he felt as trapped as her sister did. But she clapped and cheered along with the other guests once the couple had been pronounced King and Queen, and she toasted their health in spiced fire-berry juice, as was traditional.

The meal which followed was far more formal than the one they'd eaten last night and Tamsyn told herself she was pleased to sit between the Sultan of Marazad and a representative from the desert kingdom of Maraban. Glad to be miles away from Xan Constantinides and relieved she didn't have to endure his unsettling presence.

But that was a lie.

All she could think about was the Greek tycoon, and her body seemed determined to reflect her increasingly distracted thoughts. She felt as if her skin had become too tight for her body. As if her senses had suddenly become sensitised. The sound of her heart seemed amplified, its beat a million times more powerful than usual. And there was no respite from these unsettling feelings which made her feel as if she was fighting something deep inside herself. Nowhere she could escape to, because she couldn't just get up and leave in the middle of a royal wedding. She tried to chat politely to the men on either side and not glance further down the long table to where a Hollywood actress and a female member of the British royal family were giggling like schoolgirls at something Xan was saying.

She wondered how early she could decently leave, especially when a troupe of musicians started playing in the galleried ballroom next door. She knew there would be dancing after dinner because Hannah had told her so, but Tamsyn had no intention of watching couples circling the dance floor and pretending she was fine on her own. Usually, she was—mainly because she had made self-sufficiency into an art form. She never yearned for a partner because that was the only way she knew how to function. If you didn't yearn for something, you wouldn't be disappointed—and anyway, relationships were a waste of time. Experience had taught her that.

Yet tonight she keenly felt the absence of something in her life. Or rather, someone. Maybe it was the inevitable sentimentality conjured up by the wedding vows, or the realisation that Hannah was now married which was making her feel so shockingly alone. Or perhaps it was the just the realisation that there was nothing waiting for her back in England other than a pile of mounting debts.

Dabbing at her lips with a napkin, she decided to slip away, just like last night. Who would notice *her* when there were so many important guests present? She rose from her seat and was just bending to retrieve the Dior bag Hannah had insisted on lending her, when she heard a rich voice from behind.

'You're not leaving?' came the silky question.

She didn't need to turn around to know who was speaking, but prior knowledge offered no protection against her feelings and Tamsyn's heart was hammering as she straightened up to meet that mocking cobalt stare. He didn't want to talk to you last night, she reminded herself—so why not continue with that state of affairs and everyone will be happy. She gave him a tight smile. 'Oh, dear. Nobody was supposed to notice.'

'Where are you going?'

Tamsyn shrugged. *Where did he think she was going?* 'Back to my room. Or should I say—to my vast suite of rooms.'

'But the night is young.'

She opened her eyes very wide. 'I didn't think people actually said that kind of thing any more.'

He raised his brows. 'You're implying it's clichéd?'

'I suspect you're clever enough to work that one out for yourself, Mr Constantinides.'

Their gazes clashed in look which made Tamsyn feel almost *playful* and the desire to flirt was overwhelming. Yet she never flirted—she wasn't sure she even knew how. She'd always been closed up and defensive because she didn't particularly like men and she certainly didn't trust them. So how come she was suddenly playing a game she'd never played before and finding she was comfortable with it? How come she wanted to tease this darkly impressive individual and for him to tease her back? She found herself wanting to stroke her finger over the curving lines of his sensual mouth, and…and…

And she had to stop this.

Because this was dangerous. More than dangerous. Tamsyn's heart clenched with something which felt uncomfortably close to vulnerability, and that scared the hell out of her. 'I have to go,' she said.

'Not yet.' He laid his hand on her arm. 'I get the distinct feeling that I really need to change your impression of me.'

Chin lifting, she offered him a belligerent gaze. 'And why would you want to do that?'

'Call it a peace-making move in honour of your sister's wedding, if you like. Just a little light-hearted fun, that's all. And the dancing has only just started,' he observed. 'You can't possibly leave until you've had at least one dance.'

'I didn't think it was obligatory. I wasn't planning on dancing with anyone.'

An arrogant smile touched the edges of his lips. 'Not even with me?'

'Especially not with you.'

'Oh? And why not, *agape mou*? Don't you like dancing?'

His voice had deepened and the throwaway endearment in his native tongue made him even more irresistible. Tamsyn stared into his dark blue eyes. When she was younger she had thrown herself around a dance floor with the rest of them, swaying beneath the flash of lights, to the DJ's heavy beat. She had shaken her arms in the air and tossed her curls while her skin had glowed and grown hot. But she'd never been asked to dance by a devastatingly handsome man in a fancy ballroom, while wearing a silken dress which pooled around her ankles.

'Because it's a bad idea,' she prevaricated.

'Stop fighting it, Tamsyn. You know you want to dance with me,' he said with silky perception, his hand moving to the small of her back as he propelled her gently towards the dance floor.

Even then she might have stopped him had Tamsyn not glanced up at the dais and seen the newly married Sheikh looking down on them, with what looked like bemusement in his eyes. Was he surprised she was planning to dance with such an honoured guest as his rich pal? She knew Kulal didn't like her, just as she didn't like him. In fact, they'd had an almighty row before the wedding when he'd turned up on her sister's doorstep. But you had to let bygones be bygones, especially now that he was her new brother-in-law.

So why not show the Sheikh she could behave with dignity—and prove to herself that she wasn't a total social misfit? Why *shouldn't* she dance with the best-looking man in the room? With a resolute nod of her head, she allowed Xan to lead her onto the ballroom, pleased there were enough people to ensure they could just blend into the crowd. Just one dance, she told herself. One dance to fulfil her obligations and she could be off.

But life never quite conformed the way you wanted it to. One dance became two, which then somehow morphed into three, and each dance seemed to propel them closer, so that their bodies felt as if they were glued together. And Xan wasn't saying anything. Well, neither was she, come to think of it. Tamsyn blamed the loudness of the lilting music but the truth was that she couldn't think of anything she wanted to say other than something wholly inappropriate.

Like: *I love the way you make me feel when you tighten your arms around my waist like that.* Or, *could you possibly press yourself a little closer?*

Did he realise that, or did she somehow silently communicate her wishes to him? Because surely there must have been a reason—some defining moment—when Xan Constantinides thought it was perfectly acceptable for him to run his fingertips down her back in a way which even to her inexperienced self, spoke of careless intimacy. For several minutes, she let him do just that and she couldn't deny how good it felt. She began to shiver each time he made the tantalisingly slow journey from the top of her neck to the base of her spine. Her heart was hammering and the rush of heat to her face echoed the molten heat which was clenching at her sex. Yet far from being disturbed by the sultry desire she was experiencing Tamsyn was aware of an intense feeling of *relief.* Briefly she closed her eyes as she dipped her forehead to rest on his shoulder as she felt the squirm of excitement. So she wasn't frigid, after all. She could feel the things other women felt. Sweet heaven—could she feel them! It was as if someone had just flicked a switch and brought her body to life, so that every sinew and fibre was thrilling with the potent power of his proximity.

She heard him murmur something in her ear, it's meaning a mystery because it was said in Greek. But then he pushed one thigh hard against hers, as if urging her legs apart and she found her super-susceptible body obeying his silent command. Her knees widened and a sudden thrill of pleasure shot through her as she felt the pressure of his hard thigh pushing against the softness of hers. Her breasts were thrusting insistently at his chest and her knees had become all wobbly and weak. She could feel the rub of her panties over a sudden honeyed slickness and felt an insistent yearning to have him touch her there…to whisper his finger over her most intimate place. To ease that escalating ache which was making her want to squirm with frustration. She swallowed, trying to ignore the heat which was flaring in her cheek—and that was when alarm bells started ringing. What was she *doing*? After years of being purer than the driven snow, was she really planning to make a slutty spectacle of herself on the dance floor—just because some super-smooth man was pressing all the right buttons?

Removing her hands from his shoulders she flattened her palms against his chest, trying not to be distracted by the hard wall of muscle as she stared up into his face. 'What the hell do you think you're doing?' she demanded.

He didn't look the slightest bit bothered by her furious accusation as he lifted his broad shoulders in a careless shrug. 'I should have thought that was perfectly obvious.'

'So suddenly you're all over me, having ignored me all the way through dinner last night?' she accused.

'You were so combative that you deserved to be ignored,' he said softly. 'But I thought we'd agreed on a truce tonight?'

'Does…?' She swallowed, willing the erratic hammering of her pulse to subside. 'Does a truce involve you coming on to me like that, in such a public way?'

'Oh, come on, Tamsyn. Let's not be hypocritical about what just happened. I thought you were enjoying yourself.' He flickered her a slow smile. 'I know I certainly was. And most people are too busy dancing to notice how close we were getting.'

Tamsyn shook her head, aware of the swing of heavy diamond earrings against her neck and nervously she touched the sleepers to check the precious jewels were secure. Which they were—unlike her. She was one seething mass of insecurity. And fear. She mustn't discount the dominant emotion which was making her feel so scared. She felt as if she'd just stepped onto a sturdy wooden floor and it was about to give way beneath her. As if Xan Constantinides had the ability to waken something inside her—something which had been sleeping all these years. Suddenly the defiant persona she had perfected to protect herself from the kind of life her mother had lived, was in danger of crumbling before her eyes. Suddenly she was terrified of just how *exposed* he was making her feel. As if she was nothing but a bunch of sensitised nerve-endings which were jangling with hungry need. She shook her head again.

'Look, I can't do this,' she whispered. 'I'm sorry. Enjoy the rest of the party but I'm going to bed. It's going to be a long flight tomorrow and I have a double shift on Monday. Nice meeting you, Xan,' she said, and without another word she began to walk off the dance floor, aware of people turning to look at her as she hurriedly brushed past them.

Xan watched her go, caught in a rare moment of indecision, his eyes drawn to the bright shimmer of curls which cascaded like flames down her back. The voice of reason was urging him to let her go, because she was trouble. Anyone could see that. All mixed up and not his type. But the hunger of his body was more powerful than reason and he'd never had a woman walk away from him before—not like this. Was this how Hannah had snared the Sheikh—the two very ordinary Wilson sisters possessing a simple but effective strategy which would make powerful men lust after them?

Like a man hypnotised he found himself following her, mesmerised by the slender curve of her glittering bottom as she left the dance floor, surprised when she didn't look back. Not once. There was no furtive side glance to check whether he was on her tail. And *that* was exciting, too. Her steps were determined—as if she really *wanted* to get away from him. This was the chase, he realised—the chase which other men spoke of but which he'd never encountered before. He could feel the tightening of his groin and hear the wild thunder of his heart, when suddenly she disappeared from sight and he was unprepared for the disappointment which flared through him. Purposefully increasing his pace, he rounded the corner and saw her—and perhaps the sound of his footsteps was enough to make her stop and turn around—a look of bewilderment on her face, as if she was genuinely surprised to see him. As if she doubted her ability to make a man follow her.

'Xan?' she said, creasing her forehead in a frown.

'Tamsyn,' he answered, and began to walk towards her, aware of her nipples pushing hard against the crystalline bodice of her dress. As he approached, he could feel the warm rush of blood pumping through his body and in that moment he felt as if he would die if he couldn't have her.

He had reached her now and could see her darkened pupils making her green eyes appear almost black—just as the moist tremble of her lips indicated an unspoken desire to have him to crush them with his own. And he would, he thought hungrily. He would take the wildcat Tamsyn Wilson to his bed and subdue her in the most satisfactory way possible.

CHAPTER FOUR

BENEATH THE FRETWORK of lanterns lighting the palace corridor, Tamsyn's heart was thundering as she watched Xan approach, his powerful body outlined by the dark fabric of his formal suit. His face was dark too and his eyes glittered out a message of intent which started a tug of longing deep inside her. It scared and excited her and she wanted to carry on running, but something was keeping her feet fixed to the spot.

'Nobody has ever walked off and left me standing alone on the dance floor like that,' he observed huskily.

From somewhere she found a remnant of her usual flippancy. 'Oh, dear. Poor Xan. Is your ego suffering?'

'It's not my ego I'm thinking about right now,' he ground out.

Some of her composure began to slip away as Tamsyn became aware of how big and strong he looked and how it had felt to be in his arms. *Hadn't it been the most incredible sensation she'd ever experienced?*

She cleared her throat, trying to dispel her euphoric recall. 'Look, I thought I'd made my feelings clear. I'm tired and on my way to bed. I don't know why you're chasing me through the corridors as if we're a pair of kids playing cops and robbers.'

'Yes, you do. You know exactly why,' he said softly. 'Because I want you and you want me. We've wanted each other from the moment we met, Tamsyn and unless we do something about it, it's going to drive us both crazy.'

It was one of those slow motion moments and Tamsyn felt her heart leap in her chest. Like when you heard something life-changing on the news. Only this wasn't something which was happening to somebody else—it was happening to *her*. She was being propositioned by Xan Constantinides—the arrogant Greek billionaire!

Her throat grew dry as she looked at him, trying not to drink in all his dark beauty, knowing she had plenty of options available. She could call for a servant. Or carrying on walking and even if he followed, she could slam the door in his face, because instinct told her he wouldn't charge at it with a battening ram, even if he looked physically capable of doing so. But even as these thoughts flickered through her mind, she realised none of them were an option. Xan Constantinides might not like her very much—nor she him—but she couldn't deny that something had happened when he'd touched her on the dance floor.

He'd cast a spell on her. Woven some sensual kind of magic which was snaring her with invisible threads. She stared into the rugged beauty of his face, aware that this was a chance to shake off the real Tamsyn—the one who'd become brittle and defiant in order to survive. This was her opportunity to become someone else for a change. Somebody soft and dreamy and different.

'You want to kiss me,' he persisted softly. 'You want that very badly, don't you, Tamsyn?'

She wanted to deny it. To tell him that he was talking rubbish and to take his ego somewhere else. But she couldn't. She found herself lifting her eyes to his, her heart filled with foreboding and longing as she attempted a shrug which didn't quite come off. 'I suppose so,' she mumbled.

He seemed to find this amusing for his lips curved into a mocking smile. 'You suppose so?' he echoed, stepping forward to tilt her chin upwards with his finger. 'I don't think I've ever been damned with so much faint praise.'

This was Tamsyn's cue for a clever retort but right now she didn't have one because he was slowly lowering his mouth on to hers. His lips were brushing over her trembling lips and she was finding it impossible not to respond. Her hands fluttered to his shoulders for support and suddenly he was pulling her closer with effortless mastery as he deepened the kiss.

And Tamsyn just lost it.

She'd been kissed before—of course she had—but never like this. She'd only ever known the thrust of a tongue and the unwanted slick of saliva. She hadn't realised that a kiss could feel like a one-way ticket to heaven. Did her dreamy gasp startle him? Was that why he drew back, before glancing both ways down the corridor and lacing her fingers with his. 'Come with me,' he said, his voice curiously uneven.

'Come where? Where are we going?'

'Where do you think we're going?' His eyes glittered with unmistakable promise. 'I'm taking you to bed.'

His masterful and slightly callous statement should have shocked her, but it didn't. Instead it thrilled her and Tamsyn could feel her cheeks glowing as he led her through endless corridors, the click-clacking of her high heels against the marble floor the only sound she could hear above the deafening thunder of her heart. Afterwards she would try to justify her behaviour by telling herself she'd been disorientated at finding herself in a desert palace, which was only adding to the fantasy-like feel of what was happening. As if the real Tamsyn Wilson was looking down and seeing a breathlessly excited woman who couldn't wait for the powerful Greek tycoon to take her to his bed.

Lit by soft lamps, his suite was just as fancy as hers—only with a much more masculine feel. Strong scarlets and deep golds dominated the high-ceilinged room and on an inlaid desk she noticed a golden pen, studded with diamonds. A collection of horse paintings took up an entire wall and one in particular caught her eye—a black stallion with yellow flowers looped around its glistening neck, as it stood against a sunset backdrop of the stark desert. Xan didn't say anything until the heavy door had closed behind them and as he drew her into the powerful warmth of his body, Tamsyn felt her heart thunder.

'Now,' he said softly, tilting her face upwards. 'Where were we?'

For once in her life she had no smart answer. All her usual flippancy drained away from her as Tamsyn stared into the Greek's rugged features and her heart gave a great punch of delight. Yet she didn't have a clue how best to respond to him. Would he be horrified if he knew what a novice she was and should she tell him?

Did it matter?

She swallowed.

Why should it matter—and why *should* she tell

him? She couldn't be the only virgin in the history of the world and there was no shame to it—even though sometimes you were made to feel like a freak just because you'd reached the grand old age of twenty-two without ever having had sex. But then, she'd never responded to a man like this before, because no man had ever made her feel like this. And was it such a crime to want to capitalise on it? To feel like a normal woman for once, instead of someone who was made of ice from the neck down?

She tried to remember what he'd just asked her. Some flirty question about what they had just been doing and that certainly wasn't something she would be forgetting in a hurry. 'You were kissing me,' she reminded him softly.

He gave a slow smile. 'So I was,' he agreed, framing her face between his palms and looking at her for a long moment before lowering his mouth to hers, exploring her lips with a thoroughness which left her reeling.

Against the jewelled bodice of her gown Tamsyn could feel her breasts growing heavy as he reached down to whisper his thumb over her peaking nipple, lazily circling it in a way which made her moan with pleasure. She pressed her lips against his neck, feeling the rapid beat of a pulse there. As his hand began to sweep luxuriously down over her satin-covered belly, she felt another great clench of her sex and she shivered. Did he sense that already she wanted to explode with pleasure? Was that why he moved his head back to survey the rapid rise and fall of her chest.

'I think we need to get on the bed,' he said unevenly. Tamsyn wasn't known for her compliancy and when people 'suggested' something, her natural instinct was to rebel. But she found herself nodding at him like some eager little puppy. 'Okay,' she whispered, tightening her grip around his neck like the clinging tendrils of a vine. 'Let's.'

Xan felt his erection pushing almost violently against his trousers and silently he cursed, because the effect she was having on him was undeniably... *urgent*. She made him feel about fifteen years old instead of thirty-three, and while he was in such a high state of arousal it made more sense to keep movement to a minimum. So why not push her to the floor and do it to her right there, on the silken rug? It would be fast and a little bit dirty but he could rid himself of this fierce hunger which was running through his veins like a fever. His mouth hardened because that might be the perfect solution—a quick coupling to alleviate their mutual frustration and allow them to discreetly go their separate ways soon afterwards?

But something about the way she was responding to him was making such an action seem almost unsavoury. She was holding onto him as trustingly as a tiny kitten—leaving him with little choice other than to carry her across the room in a macho display which wasn't really his style. He was taken aback by how shockingly *primitive* the gesture made him feel as another spear of lust shafted through him.

Bemusement filled him as he set her down beside the brocade-covered divan, because Tamsyn Wilson wasn't turning out to be what he'd expected. In fact, none of this was what he'd expected. She was confounding him with mixed messages. The street-wise minx was behaving in a way which was almost *naïve*.

He'd imagined that someone so sassy and sexy would by now be unzipping him, before taking him boldly in her hand, or her mouth—because that seemed to be the current trend for first time sex. The cynic in him often wondered if this was the moment when women attempted to showcase their sexual skills in as short a time as possible—rather like a job applicant deftly running through their entire resume on a first interview. But not Tamsyn. She seemed more concerned with removing those ostentatious diamond earrings and finding a low table beside the bed on which to safely put them, quickly followed by the glittering diamond choker. And while she was turning round to do that, he moved behind her, lifting the thick curtain of her curls to drift his lips over her neck. He felt her tremble then slump against him and she wondered if she could feel his hardness pressing into her bottom.

'I want you,' he said, very deliberately, as he turned her round to face him.

'D-do you?' she said, her voice barely a whisper.

How did she manage to sound so convincingly *shy*, he wondered? Pulling a couple of clips from her hair, he unzipped her gown so that it slithered to the ground in a pool of glittering silk and net and she was left standing in nothing but her bra and panties. He felt another kick of desire. Her legs were bare and he bent before her to remove one silver shoe, quickly followed by another, but when he stood up again he was taken aback by how tiny she seemed without the towering heels.

Shrugging off his jacket and yanking off his tie, he let them fall to join her discarded dress. 'Unbutton my shirt,' he growled.

Tamsyn's fingers were trembling as she lifted them to Xan's chest, because for all her bravado she'd never seen a man naked and she'd certainly never undressed anyone before. Yet her instinctive fear was banished by that first sweet touch of the skin which sheathed his hard muscle and she heard him groan as the buttons flew open. Now what, she wondered, as she gazed at his bare chest—too daunted to think about attacking the zip of his trousers.

Did he sense her sudden nervousness? Was that why he gave another slow smile and unclipped her front-fastening bra so that her breasts spilled into his waiting palms and suddenly her nerves were all but forgotten? She writhed as his thumbs circled her nipples and her excitement grew as he moved his hand down between her thighs. Pushing aside the damp, stretched panel at her crotch, he found her slick heat, sliding his finger against the engorged bud with practised ease. And this was *heaven*. Her hips were circling of their own accord and she was moaning now and the part of her brain which was urging her to be careful, was abruptly silenced by the most powerful desire she could ever have imagined.

'Xan...' she breathed, looking up to meet the smoky lust which had narrowed his eyes.

'You are just as hot as I thought you'd be,' he declared unevenly.

She should have said something then, but she couldn't even think of the words—let alone form a sentence with them—not when he was laying her down on the bed and pulling off the rest of his clothes with unsteady hands. And then he was naked—his body warm and strong as he lay down beside her. His hungry kiss was fuelling this wild new hunger which was spiralling up inside her and suddenly Tamsyn was on fire. His lips were on her breasts and her belly—tantalising her until she thought she would go out of her mind. And when he guided her hand to his groin, there was no shyness as she encountered the hard ridge of his erection. Instead, she felt nothing but joy as she began to whisper her fingertips against it. But he shook his head as he reached for something on the nightstand and she heard the little tear of foil and realised he must be sheathing himself.

This was it. The moment she'd never thought she'd reach because she had always been unresponsive and afraid. But she wasn't afraid now as he moved over her and spread her legs apart. Not even when she felt that brief burst of pain and momentarily, he stilled. Instinct told her to angle her hips and to propel them forward so that he slid inside her completely—and once her body had grown accustomed to his width—those incredible sensations of pleasure were back. And how. She cried out with it so that he stilled once again and his words came out clipped, like bullets.

'I am hurting you?'

'No. No. Not at all. It's…*oh!* Oh, Xan. It's heaven.'

'Is it now? Then I had just better…. *Do. It. Some. More.*'

With each emphasised word, he thrust deeper and deeper, until her nails were digging into his back. Tamsyn could feel the build-up of something. Something so delicious she didn't believe it could get any better, except that it did. And then better still. It was like being whizzed to the top of a high tower block and being told to jump off, and willingly she did, gasping out his name in an expression of disbelief as she went flying over some sunlight ledge.

As he heard the helpless sound of her cries, Xan knew he couldn't hold back. Not a second longer. And when his orgasm came it left him shaken. His head fell back and it took several breathless minutes before he could distance himself by rolling away from her. Because he needed to do that. He needed to make sense of what had just happened—even though all he could think about was the folly of what he'd just done.

He had seduced the Sheikh's sister-in-law!

And against all the odds, she had been a *virgin*.

He stared down at her, at where her magnificent hair tumbled like fire against the muddled pile of pillows. Her eyes were closed though experience told him she was not asleep, though he suspected she wanted him to think she was. But she was in his room and he wanted answers.

Now.

'That was some…surprise,' he drawled.

She opened her eyes and he steeled himself against their beauty, but somehow they had lost their luminous quality. They looked as flat as pieces of jade as she returned his stare and he could see her dreamy expression being replaced with her more usual look of rebellion.

'What, that the woman you'd clearly slotted into the category of "she'll be up for anything", turned out to be less experienced than you imagined?' she challenged.

He made a growling little sound at the back of his throat. 'Didn't you think it was a big enough deal to tell me I was your first lover?' he demanded. 'Or that it might be the *polite* thing to have done?'

At this, Tamsyn nearly burst out laughing. 'Polite? We haven't exactly been polite to each other up until now, have we?' she retorted. 'At what point *exactly* was I supposed to tell you? You'll forgive me if I don't know the protocol for this kind occasion.'

'Well, neither do I!'

'Are you saying that I'm the first virgin you've ever had sex with?'

'*Neh*... Yes,' he translated.

There was a moment of silence. '*Why*?'

'Why do you think?' he questioned sarcastically. 'If someone your age has waited all this time to have sex, it's usually an indication of her having unrealistic expectations.'

'Such as?'

He shrugged. 'Holding out for a wedding ring is the first thing which springs to mind.'

'You really are the most arrogant man I've ever met.'

'I don't deny it,' he said, unabashed. 'But at least you can't accuse me of being dishonest.'

But wasn't there a part of Tamsyn which wished he had been? A previously unknown side of herself which longed for him to tell her that it had been wonderful and she was wonderful, and from now on she was going to be his girlfriend.

Had she taken *complete* leave of her senses?

She needed to face the facts, like she'd always done. She'd just had sex, that was all. It might not have been the smartest move to chose Xan Constantinides as her first lover but she wasn't going to deny how superb he'd been. And what she was *not* going to do was to regret it. Didn't she have enough regrets already, without adding one more to the list? Couldn't she take pleasure from the most amazing thing which had ever happened to her, without carrying around a whole shedload of guilt?

She shifted her weight again and the slippery golden sheet slithered away to her breast and suddenly he was saying something in thick and urgent Greek before pulling her hungrily into his arms. Maybe Tamsyn should have been daunted by the newly massive erection she felt pressing against her belly but she wasn't—mainly because she was remembering what had just happened. And she wanted it to happen all over again.

Eagerly she raised her face to search for his kiss, feeling a shiver of excitement rippling uncontrollably through her body as the Greek billionaire reached blindly for a second condom.

CHAPTER FIVE

TAMSYN HAD HEARD plenty about the 'walk of shame' but she'd never experienced it before. The furtive walk from a man's bedroom back to your own, wearing last night's clothes and praying that nobody would notice you. But how on earth was she going to manage that when she was wearing *full evening dress*?

Tamsyn quickly realised it was a naïve and futile hope. Not only did she pass countless servants silently scurrying through the sunlit corridors—she even had the misfortune to encounter a large group of wedding guests who were clearly being given an early-morning guided tour by one of the Sheikh's assistants. It would have been almost comical to see their reaction to her sudden appearance, if it had been happening to anyone other than her.

The guide's voice faded away and everyone's mouths fell open as a barefooted Tamsyn rounded the corner, wearing a now crumpled grey evening dress and dangling her silver high-heeled shoes from one hand, while her other tightly grasped a pair of priceless diamond earrings and a matching choker. The guide seemed to recover himself—maybe he recognised her as the Sheikh's new sister-in-law—because he cleared his throat and gave a strangled kind of smile.

'You are lost, mistress?'

Tamsyn gave a thin smile. Yes, she was lost—but only in the emotional sense of the word, and once again wondered what on earth had possessed her to indulge in a long night of sex with a man she instinctively sensed was dangerous.

You know why. Because you couldn't stop yourself. Because the moment he touched you, you went up in flames.

Ignoring the knowing side glances of the men and the hostile glare of the women in the group, Tamsyn gave a determined shake of her head, making her unbrushed curls fly around her shoulders like angry red corkscrews. 'I'm just on my way back to my room,' she said cheerily. 'It seemed a pity not to get up early and watch the sun rise over the desert.'

They obviously didn't believe a word she was saying, but since she would never see them again after today—who cared?

She made it back to her room at last, tearing off her dress, throwing aside the shoes and carefully putting the jewellery down, before escaping into the sanctuary of the luxurious bathroom. At least the steam of the hot shower and the rich lather of perfumed soap made her feel marginally better, but not for long, because flashback images kept coming back to haunt her. Imagines of a hard, muscular body driving down on hers and warm arms enfolding her and holding her tight. *Just concentrate on what you're supposed to be doing*, she told herself fiercely as she dragged a brush through her unruly curls. She had just slithered into her old denim cut-offs and a clean T-shirt, when there was a rap at the door.

She wasn't going to deny the leap of her heart in response, or the determined pep talk she gave herself as she walked across the palatial suite. She told herself to play it cool. If Xan Constantinides wanted her phone number then she would give it to him, but she wasn't going to act like it was a big deal. She might never have had sex before but over the years she'd listened to how friends and colleagues dealt with the thorny issue of The Morning After. And apparently the most stupid thing a woman could ever do, was to come over all eager.

Composing her face into what she hoped wasn't an over-the-top smile, it faded immediately when she opened the door to discover it wasn't Xan standing there but the newly crowned Queen of Zahristan—her sister Hannah! A sister whose face was filled with anger as she walked in without waiting to be invited, pushing the door shut behind her, before assuming a grim expression of accusation which Tamsyn recognised all too well.

'Would you like to tell me what's going on?' she demanded.

'I could ask the same thing of you!' retorted Tamsyn, reframing the accusation and turning it on its head since attack was always the best form of defence. 'It's the first day of your honeymoon—so what are you doing barging into my bedroom at this time in the morning? Won't your new husband be wondering where you are?'

Hannah bit her lip and Tamsyn was shocked to see the despair which briefly darkened her sister's eyes because she was usually cheerful, no matter what life threw at her. And despite her own predicament, Tamsyn felt her heart plummet as her worst fears began to materialise. Was Hannah's marriage already starting to go off the rails, even though she had only been crowned Queen the previous day? She had warned her sister that it was a mistake to marry such a man as arrogant as Kulal. She'd begged her not to go through with the marriage just because she was pregnant, but Hannah hadn't listened. What if the powerful Sheikh was being cruel to his pregnant wife—what then?

'So where's Kulal, Hannah?' Tamsyn probed, as suspicion continued to stab at her heart like a dagger. 'Doesn't he mind you being here, quizzing me, on the first morning of his honeymoon?'

'I'm not here to talk about my relationship!' declared Hannah, but Tamsyn could hear the sorrow in her voice. 'I'm here to ask whether you spent the night with Xan Constantinides.'

And despite all her bravado, Tamsyn felt a shiver whisper over her skin. Was it hearing someone else say the words out loud which drove home the true nature of what she had done? After years of fiercely guarding her innocence she had let the Greek tycoon lead her back to his suite and take her virginity with barely an arrogant snap of his fingers. A man she barely knew. A man she would probably never see again.

And it had been the most amazing thing which had ever happened to her.

They had spent the night having passionate sex—over and over again. He'd said things to her in Greek she hadn't understood and things to her in English which she had, and which made her blush just remembering them.

'You drive me crazy. Your breasts are small but the most perfect I have ever seen,' he had growled at one point, lifting his head from her nipple, where the lick of his tongue and the graze of his teeth had been enough to have her writhing on the bed in ecstasy. 'And do you want to know what else about you is perfect?'

She remembered thinking how delectable he looked with his cheekbones all flushed and his black hair wild as a lion's mane from where she'd been running her fingers through it. She remembered an instinctive feeling of sexual power flooding through her as she met his hectic cobalt gaze. 'Yes,' she whispered. 'Yes, I do.'

But he had answered with the urgent thrust of his seemingly ever-present erection, and Tamsyn had almost passed with pleasure as he brought her hurtling over the edge of fulfilment, again and again and again.

She must have fallen asleep eventually, because when she opened her eyes it had been to discover herself alone in the rumpled bed with bright sunlight on her face and only a scrawled note occupying the space where Xan had lain. She had picked it up with trembling fingers and read it.

> *Gone riding in the desert. That was the most perfect night.*
> *Thank you.*
> *Xan.*

Tamsyn's heart had sunk for it had read like the farewell it was obviously intended to be. There had been no line of kisses. No phone number or email address, or invitation to have dinner with him back in London.

Well, what had she been expecting—everlasting love?

Of course she hadn't, but even facing up to the folly of her actions didn't make it any easier. She'd done some pretty stupid things in her time, but sleeping with Xan Constantinides must rank right up there with some of the worst decisions she'd ever made. Easy come, easy go—that was probably how he saw it. If you slept with a man without even going out on a formal date, then why would he treat you with respect? Tamsyn swallowed. Was she doomed to follow the path laid down by her own mother, despite her determination to live her life in a very different way?

Now she stared into Hannah's aquamarine eyes which were so unlike her own. She guessed they each carried a legacy from their different fathers—both useless in their different ways—and fleetingly she wondered whether that was why they'd both made such bad choices when choosing men. Except that she hadn't chosen Xan—he had chosen her.

And he had done a runner as soon as possible.

She shrugged her shoulders with a familiar gesture of defiance. 'Yes, I spent the night with Xan Constantinides.'

'But Tamsyn, *why*?'

For the first time Tamsyn felt like smiling as she looked at her sister. Her pale-faced sister with dark shadows under her eyes. 'You're honestly asking me that? You might be a married woman now—but surely you're not completely immune to the charms of a man like Xan Constantinides.'

At the mention of marriage, Hannah flinched. 'No, of course I'm not,' she said quietly. 'And that's precisely why he's the wrong kind of man for you, Tamsyn. He might be obscenely good-looking and have the kind of sex appeal which should carry a public health warning, but he's known for his...his...'

'His *what*?' prompted Tamsyn, though her heart was smashing against her rib cage because she guessed what was coming.

'Let's just say he *enjoys* women! He enjoys them very much.'

'I wasn't expecting him to be celibate!'

Hannah sucked in a long breath, her face growing serious. 'It's more than that. He usually dates actresses. Or models. Or heiresses.'

'Not waitresses on short-term contracts who are always getting fired for insubordination, you mean?' offered Tamsyn drily.

'And you...'

Tamsyn watched as Hannah unconsciously rubbed her enormous gold and ruby wedding band, as if reaffirming to herself that she really *was* married. And once again she wondered why her sister was standing *here* on the first morning of her honeymoon, looking like the very opposite of what a glowing newlywed should be. Why wasn't she romping in bed with her husband? 'I what, Hannah?'

The new Queen chewed on her lip. 'I know you were inexperienced with men, Tamsyn,' she breathed. 'And by associating with someone like Xan, you're operating right out of your league.

'Oh, don't worry,' Tamsyn assured her airily. 'I'm

not anticipating any kind of future with him. I'm not *that* stupid.'

'But what...' Hannah sucked in a deep breath. 'What if you're pregnant?'

Tamsyn knew she didn't have to have this conversation, no matter how close the two sisters had been when they were growing up. But in a way she *did* need to have it, because wouldn't voicing her inner fears help put them into perspective? Like when you had a terrible nightmare and the shadows in the room seemed to symbolise all kinds of terrible things—yet when you put a lamp on you soon saw that the imagined monster was a chair, or a dressing table.

'We used protection,' she said quietly.

Hannah's eyes were very big. 'So did we,' she whispered. 'And look what happened.'

And suddenly Tamsyn was made very aware of how easily a woman could be trapped by her own passion. Hannah had accidently become pregnant by the Sheikh which was why she had married him. Who was to say the same thing wouldn't happen to her? She found herself uttering a small, silent prayer. 'We'll just have to hope it doesn't happen to me,' she said quietly.

'And what if it does?'

'Then I'll deal with it. But I'm not going to project like that. I'm just going to carry on as before.'

'Doing what?'

Tamsyn patted the back pocket of her cut-offs to check she had her cellphone. 'Doing what I always do. Adapting. Moving on.'

Distractedly, Hannah began to pace up and down the room, the silken shimmer of her flowing robes seeming to emphasise the growing differences between them. Stopping in front of one of the tall windows which overlooked the palace gardens, the streaming sunlight had turned her pale blonde hair into liquid gold and Tamsyn thought how scarily royal she looked. 'Kulal says we might be able to find a role for you in the London Embassy.'

'As what? The new attaché?' enquired Tamsyn, deadpan.

'I'm serious, Tamsyn. There are always cleaning jobs available—or we thought you might like to help the chef in the Ambassador's private kitchen.' Hannah gave a somewhat helpless shrug. 'Something like that.'

'Well, thanks but no thanks,' said Tamsyn firmly. 'I don't want to be beholden to your husband and I'd prefer to make my own way in life, just like I've always done.'

At this, Hannah walked forward to place her hand on Tamsyn's arm. 'But if anything *happens*,' she said fervently. 'If you find out you *are* pregnant—then you will come to me for help, won't you, Tamsyn?'

'If I were you, I think I'd be concentrating on your life rather than mine,' said Tamsyn sharply. 'I've never seen you looking so pale. What's the matter, Hannah—have you suddenly discovered there are serpents in paradise?'

Was her remark too close to the bone? Was that why Hannah's face crumpled and she looked as if she was about to cry? Tamsyn felt a sudden pang of guilt as her sister turned towards the arched doorway, but any remorse was quickly cancelled out by the enormity of what her sister had just said to her. Because that was something she hadn't even considered. Her stomach performed a sickly somersault as Hannah left the room and Tamsyn stared unseeingly at one of the priceless silken rugs. What if Hannah's fears were true? What if she *was* pregnant?

She tried to put it—and him—out of her mind, though it wasn't easy on the flight back to England. Especially when the stewardess had answered her studiedly casual query about Xan by informing her that Mr Constantinides had summoned his own jet and left Zahristan earlier that morning.

But the anxious wait to discover if she was carrying his baby was even harder when she was back in London and the whole thing seemed like a dream. Tamsyn tried all kinds of coping mechanisms. Just like she'd promised Hannah, she threw herself into her latest job—working in a steam-filled café in one of the tiny back roads near Covent Garden, which was mainly frequented by taxi drivers. It wasn't the best-paid work she'd ever done and it certainly wasn't the most exciting. She suspected it had been called The Greasy Spoon in an ironic sense, though it certainly lived up to is name since no meal was served unless it was swimming in its own pool of oil. But she wasn't going to waste hours hunting for some rewarding position which was never going to materialise. She needed to be *busy*—doing something other than neurotically ticking off the endlessly long days as she waited for her period. She needed to focus on something other than the fact that her first and only lover had not bothered to seek her out—not even to enquire whether she had arrived home safely.

She hated the way she kept glancing at her phone. Even though she hadn't given him her number, hadn't part of her thought—*hoped*—that the Greek tycoon might have somehow tracked her down? It wasn't outside the realms of possibility that he could have asked the Sheikh, was it? But deep down Tamsyn knew she was clutching at straws and it was never going to happen. For a man to go to the trouble of finding you, he had to like you enough to want to see you again. And you certainly didn't have to *like* a woman in order to have sex with her.

But she wasn't going to beat herself up about it. She hadn't planned on being intimate with Xan, but she hadn't planned to be a virgin for ever either. She had been waiting—not for a wedding band, because marriage was something she simply wasn't interested in. No. She had been waiting for someone to make her feel desire—real, bone-melting desire—even though she'd secretly thought it would never happen. Yet it had. Xan Constantinides might not be a keeper, but she wasn't deluded enough to deny that he'd had a profound effect on her.

So she tried to be practical rather than wistful. She would probably see him again at the naming ceremony of Kulal and Hannah's baby, sometime in the not too distant future. And before that happened, she would need to school herself in the art of pretending not to care. If she worked on it hard enough, she might actually have achieved that blissful state by then. Her heart pounded. And if she *was* pregnant, what then? Then the world would look like a very different place.

But then her period arrived and for some inexplicable reason, she cried and cried. But not for long, because she knew tears were a waste of energy. She just carried on getting up every morning and going to work. It was dark when she started and dark when she finished and although spring was just around the corner, the bitter wind was harsh and unremitting.

And then she had one of those days when everything seemed to go wrong. A customer queried his change, causing the sharp-eyed manageress to watch her like a hawk, which made Tamsyn clumsier than usual. Outside, heavy rain was bashing against the window, making the steamed-up café resemble a sauna, and some inane pop quiz was blaring from the radio, the words incomprehensible above the laddish shouts of conversation. She had just muddled up two egg orders and was anticipating the kind of stern lecture which usually preceded being asked to leave a job, when the doorbell tinged and unusually, the whole place became silent.

Tamsyn looked up as a reverential hush fell over the boisterous customers and she had another of those slow motion moments. Because it was Xan. Xan Constantinides was walking into the crowded café and every single eye in the place was fixed on him.

She wasn't surprised. Not just because his costly clothes proclaimed his billionaire status, it was more the sense that he was a super-being—somehow larger than life and more good-looking than anyone had a right to be. His rain-spattered dark overcoat was made of fine cashmere and she doubted whether any other Greasy Spoon customer had ever worn handmade shoes, or moved with such a powerful sense of purpose.

She hated the instinctive ripple of recognition which shivered through her body. Hated the sudden clench of her nipples beneath the manmade fabric of her uniform. He was walking towards her, those cobalt eyes fixed firmly on hers and Tamsyn was doing her best to look at him with the kind of politely questioning smile she would give to any other customer, even though she wanted to spit venom at him. But the manageress was literally elbowing her out of the way, surreptitiously patting the bright red perm which the steam had turned to frizz, her fifty-year-old face filled with the gushing excitement of a schoolgirl as she stepped forward.

'Can I 'elp you, sir?'

Was Xan clued-up enough to realise the power structure which was being acted out in front of him? Was that why he turned the full wattage of his incredible smile on the manageress? Or maybe that's just what came naturally, thought Tamsyn disgustedly. Maybe he used his remarkable charisma as a means to an end, no matter where he was.

'You certainly can,' said Xan, his honeyed Greek accent sounding almost obscenely erotic. 'I was wondering if I might borrow Tamsyn for a little while?'

The woman's smile instantly turned into a grimace. 'She doesn't finish her shift until seven,' she answered unhelpfully.

And that was when Tamsyn piped up—and to hell with the consequences. She stared at Xan, determined not to be affected by the gleam of his gaze as she tried desperately to forget the last time she'd seen that powerful body. Yet how could she forget all that olive-skinned splendour as he'd held her tightly in his arms? Or discount the temporary sanctuary he'd provided as he rocked in and out of her body all night?

And then he had left her. Had walked away as if she didn't exist. Left her open to pain and self-doubt. Was she going to keep coming back for more?

'You can't *borrow* me,' she snapped. 'I'm not a book you take from the library.'

'Tamsyn! I will not have you speaking to a customer like that!' the manageress cut in, revelling in the opportunity to administer a public telling-off.

'Please.' Xan's intervention was smooth. 'It's no problem. I can see you're very busy here and unable to spare her. I'll come back at seven, if that's okay.'

Tamsyn wanted to scream at them to stop talking about her as if she wasn't in the room, because hadn't that been what all those case-workers used to do when they held those interminable meetings to discover why she kept bunking off school? And she wanted her stupid, betraying body to stop reacting to the Greek. She didn't *want* to look at the sensual curve of his lips and be reminded of how it had felt to have him kiss her. 'I'm busy at seven,' she said.

The cobalt eyes narrowed. 'Really?'

'Really.' It was a lie, but Tamsyn didn't care—because surely a small white lie was preferable to doing or saying something you might later regret. And she didn't owe him *anything*.

'Then when are you free?' he persisted.

'I'm not,' Tamsyn answered. 'There's absolutely nothing I want to say to you, Xan. It's over. You made that perfectly clear. So if you'll excuse me—the kitchen has just rung the bell with another order.'

And with that, she marched over to the aluminium serving hatch to pick up the bacon butty which was already growing cold.

CHAPTER SIX

STANDING HUDDLED IN a shop doorway opposite the now dark café, Xan waited for Tamsyn to emerge but it was already ten after seven and still she hadn't shown.

The shop doorway remained defiantly closed and he wondered if perhaps she'd slipped away unseen from the back of the building. He wondered what lengths she would go to in order to avoid him.

He'd imagined...

What?

That she would be deliriously happy to see him, despite him having failed to contact her after their passionate night at the palace? Despite the fact that he'd hired a private jet to get away from Zahristan as quickly as possible the next morning, after leaving her only the briefest of notes, and then had disappeared for the best part of three months?

Yes. That's exactly what he'd imagined because it had happened so often before. Women took whatever crumbs he was prepared to offer them. They were grateful for anything they got and even when they complained it wasn't enough, they still came back for more. He'd meant it when he'd told Tamsyn he wasn't deliberately cruel—despite the tearful accusations sometimes hurled at him in the past. He was just genuinely detached. He'd learnt detachment from the moment he'd left the womb—that was one of the inevitable legacies of having a mother who was so bogged down with self-pity that she barely deigned to notice her child. He never raised hopes unnecessarily, or proceeded with a relationship if the odds were stacked against it. And breaking the heart of his friend's new sister-in-law was never going to be on the cards.

He shouldn't have bedded her in the first place which was why he hadn't hung around the day after the wedding. Why he'd deliberately avoided seeing her and instead gone riding with the Sheikh, who had seemed to have enough problems of his own without Xan adding to them.

He had waited for the dust to settle and his libido to cool and for a short period of time to elapse. Then he had flown out to his beautiful waterfront estate in Argolida on the Peloponnese Peninsula, to begin the future which had been mapped out for him so long ago. There had been several meetings with the young woman he'd once agreed to marry and he had gone through the motions of what was expected of him. It should have been simple, but it had turned out to be anything but. He had stumbled at the first hurdle—he who never stumbled. Failure wasn't a word which featured in his vocabulary and for weeks he had attempted to cajole then scold himself into a state of acceptance—an acceptance which had stubbornly refused to materialise. He'd witnessed Sofia's bewilderment as he struggled to find the right things to say. He had pictured his father's distress when he explained that the marriage was a no-go he should never have agreed to. For the first time in his life he hadn't known which way to turn. If he married Sofia he could not make her happy, but if he walked away—what then? Her pride would be wounded and his family's reputation tarnished.

It had been at the beginning of a conference call with the Sheikh last week that a solution had suddenly occurred to Xan. It wasn't perfect—but then, what in life could be regarded as perfect? But it would suffice. It would have to. And surely it was better than the alternative.

His throat dried as the café door swung open and Tamsyn stepped out into the rainy night and suddenly every thought drained from his mind. Yet why should his heart race like a train when she was dressed so unbecomingly? In her faded jeans and ugly padded jacket, she shouldn't have merited a second glance. But something seemed to happen to his vision whenever Tamsyn Wilson was around and he found himself unable to tear his eyes away from her. It had happened the first time he'd laid eyes on her but it was a whole lot worse now. Was it because, despite her sassiness and outspokenness, she had been an innocent virgin—thus defying all his jaded expectations? He kept replaying that moment when he'd first penetrated her sweet tightness and she'd made that choking little cry, her mouth open and moist as it had sucked helplessly against his shoulder.

Her hair was tied back, her ponytail flowing behind her like a curly red banner, but her face was pale. So pale. From here you couldn't see the freckles which spattered her skin like gold. He found himself remembering the ones which reposed in the soft flesh of her inner thighs. How he had whispered his tongue over them…tantalising and teasing her, before bringing her to yet another jerking orgasm, which had left her shuddering against his mouth.

He began to walk towards her, aided by the red gleam of the traffic lights which was reflecting off the wet road like spilled blood. And then she saw him, her eyes first widening and then narrowing as she put her head down and increased her speed and Xan felt a flicker of excitement as he realised she was trying to get away from him, just like she'd done at the palace. Did she really think she would outpace him? Didn't she realise he'd seen the yearning look of hunger in her eyes when he'd walked into that steamy café, and it had echoed the hunger in him?

'Tamsyn!'

'Can't you take a hint?' she shouted back over her shoulder. 'Just go *away*, Xan!'

She didn't slow down as he followed her along the wet pavement but he caught her up easily enough, his long strides easily outperforming her small, rapid steps. 'We need to talk,' he said, as he caught up with her.

She stopped then. Lifted up her chin to glare at him and the raindrops glistened like diamonds on her freckled skin as she stood beneath the golden flare of the streetlamp.

'But that's where you're wrong!' she contradicted fervently. 'We don't *need* to do anything. Why would we when there's nothing between us? Didn't you make it plain that's what you wanted when you slipped out of bed that morning, taking great care not to wake me?'

'Why?' he parried softly. 'Did you want there to be something between us?'

'In your dreams!' she declared. 'Even if I did want to get involved with a man—which I don't—you're the last person on the planet I'd ever choose! I already told you that.'

A low sigh of relief escaped from his lips and some of the tension left him. 'That's probably the best news I've heard all week,' he said. 'And yet another reason why we need to have a conversation.'

Tamsyn steeled herself against the sexy dip in his voice, brushing the rain away from her cheeks with an impatient fist. 'You just don't get it, do you?' she hissed. 'I'm not interested in what you've got to say, Xan. I've just been sacked and it's all your fault.'

His eyebrows shot up. '*My* fault?'

'Yes! If you hadn't come into the cafe—swaggering around the place as if you owned it and demanding I take a break I wasn't entitled to—then I'd still have a job. Your attitude made me so angry so that I answered you back, giving that witch of a manageress the ideal opportunity to tell me not to bother coming back tomorrow.'

'So that's the only reason you were fired?' he questioned slowly.

Tamsyn told herself she didn't have to answer. That she owed him nothing—and certainly not an explanation. Yet it was difficult to withstand the perceptive gleam in his eyes or not to be affected by the sudden understanding that since Hannah had gone away to live in the desert, she really *was* on her own. That once again she was jobless, with nobody to turn to—with outstanding rent to pay on her overpriced bedsit. Giving a suddenly deflated sigh, she shrugged, all the energy needed to maintain the fiction of her life suddenly draining away. 'Not the only reason, no,' she agreed reluctantly. 'I guess I'm fundamentally unsuited to being a waitress.'

Beneath the streetlight, his eyes gleamed. 'All the more reason for you to have dinner with me, since I have a proposition to put to you which you might find interesting.'

The suggestion was so unexpected that Tamsyn blinked. 'What sort of proposition?'

Tiny droplets of rain flew like diamonds from the tangle of his ebony hair as he shook his head. 'This isn't a conversation to have in the rain. Let's find a restaurant where we can talk.'

Her stomach chose that moment to make an angry little rumble and Tamsyn realised she hadn't eaten since breakfast. She told herself it was hunger which made her consider his suggestion—it definitely wasn't because she was reluctant to see him walk out of her life for a second time. But then she looked at her damp jeans and realised what a mess she looked. 'I can't possibly go out looking like this.'

'You could go home first and get changed.' He gave a small inclination of his head. 'I have a car here.'

Tamsyn stiffened as a black limousine began to drive slowly towards them. Was he out of his mind? Did he really think she'd let someone like him within a mile of her scrubby little bedsit? She could just imagine the shock on his over-privileged face if he caught sight of the damp walls and the electric kettle which was covered in lime-scale. 'I live miles away.'

'Then let's just go to the Granchester.'

Tamsyn nearly choked as he casually mentioned the exclusive hotel where her sister used to work before being fired for sleeping with one of the guests. 'The Granchester is just about the most expensive hotel in London,' she objected. 'We'll never be able to get a table at this short notice, and even if we could there's no way I could go somewhere like that for dinner, wearing this.'

'Oh, we'll a get a table,' he said smoothly, as the limousine drew up beside them. 'And my cousin's wife Emma is staying there at the moment. You look about the same size as her. She'll lend you something to wear.'

Tamsyn shook her head. 'Don't be so ridiculous. I can't possibly borrow a dress from a complete stranger!'

'Of course you can.' He spoke with the confidence of someone unused to being thwarted, as he opened the door of the car and gently pushed her inside. 'Don't worry. I'll fix it.'

Afterwards Tamsyn would put her uncharacteristic compliance down to his distracting presence, or maybe it was just his sheer *certainty*. She'd never experienced the sensation of a man taking control of a situation in such an unflappable way. She wasn't used to someone offering to *fix* things. She was used to drama and chaos. She wondered if there was some biological chink in her armour which made her yield to his superior strength, or whether she'd just had the stuffing knocked out of her by the loss of yet another job? Either way, she found herself climbing into the back of the taxi with Xan sliding next to her as they began to drive at speed through the rain, towards the Granchester.

The rain-blurred lights of the city passed in a streak while Xan made a phone call. She heard him say her name as he began speaking in rapid Greek, before laughing at something the person on the end of the line must have said. And it was the laugh which made Tamsyn's heart clench with unexpected wistfulness. Imagine living the kind of life where you could just jump into the back of a limousine without worrying about the cost, and laugh so uninhibitedly as you chatted on the phone—as if you didn't have a care in the world.

Like a glittering citadel, the Granchester Hotel rose up before them and as the car slid to a halt, a doorman sprang forward to greet Xan like an old friend. The flower-filled foyer was busy as expensively dressed guests milled around, looking as if they had somewhere important to go. A woman was walking purposefully towards them, one of the most beautiful women Tamsyn had ever seen. Slim and smiling, her hair was as pale as moonlight and she was wearing a short blue dress which hugged her hips and a tiny cardigan just a shade darker.

'Xan!' she said fondly, rising up on the toes of her ballet pumps to kiss the Greek tycoon on both cheeks, before turning to Tamsyn with a wide smile. 'And you must be Tamsyn,' she said. 'I'm Emma and I'm married to Xan's cousin. I gather you need something to wear for dinner tonight and time is tight—so why don't you come with me and I can sort you something out?'

It was weird—maybe because Emma was so polite and so...*gracious*—that Tamsyn didn't find herself frozen by her usual air of suspicion. Instead, she smiled back and the three of them walked over to an elevator which nobody else seemed to be using. And of course, the presence of Emma in the enclosed space meant that Tamsyn's conversation with Xan was temporarily interrupted, although she couldn't help but be acutely aware of his presence and the mocking light in his eyes. What on earth have I got myself into? she wondered as the elevator slid to a silent halt and they stepped directly into an enormous room whose wall to ceiling windows gave a stunning view over the glittering skyscrapers of London.

'Xan, why don't you help yourself to a drink?' Emma gave another soft smile. 'Tamsyn, come with me.'

In a dream-like state, Tamsyn followed the elegant blonde down a long corridor and into a dressing room which led off from an huge bedroom. Maybe if she hadn't just lost her job for the umpteenth time and maybe if the image of her tiny bedsit hadn't just flashed into her mind, then she might have told Emma she'd changed her mind, thanked her for her kind offer and just left. Xan might be keen to put some mysterious 'proposition' to her, but despite what she suspected was his tendency to always get his own way—she doubted whether he would actually try to keep her here by force.

But she didn't do any of those things. Perhaps it was the blonde's serene presence or just the fact that Tamsyn was tired. Bone tired. As if she could sleep for a hundred years and then maybe a hundred more. So she nodded politely as Emma ran her perfectly manicured fingernails—a deep shade of blue which matched her cardigan—along a line of colour-co-ordinated clothes hanging in the biggest closet Tamsyn had ever seen.

'I'm not going to stand over you and influence your choice,' she told Tamsyn softly. 'Just wear whatever takes your fancy—and that includes shoes, if they fit. I'll go and entertain your man and see you back in the sitting room.'

Mutely, Tamsyn nodded. She wanted to tell Emma that Xan wasn't her anything but surely that was an over-complicating factor and things were complicated enough already. Her heart was racing as she quickly washed in the en-suite bathroom before slithering into a long-sleeved dress in green cashmere which she cinched in at the waist with a belt. Her tiny feet swam like boats in tall Emma's sleek footwear so she packed the toes of some green suede shoes with wads of tissue paper. Liberating her curls from their elastic band, she raked a comb through them in a vain attempt to tame them and, tucking her own damp clothes under her arm, walked back towards the sitting room.

She was surprised to hear Emma speaking in Greek to Xan, but the conversation died away as she walked into the massive room. She couldn't deny the inordinate amount of pleasure she took from the look of disbelief on Xan's face as slowly he looked her up and down. It reminded her that she really *could* scrub up well—even if she had to rely on the charity of other people in order to do so.

The tycoon was rising to his feet, dominating the room with his powerful presence, a faint smile curving his lips. 'I've told Emma we have a table booked downstairs.'

It seemed almost rude to just *use* the kind blonde's

apartment like some kind of upmarket changing room, but Emma was also getting to her feet, giving Tamsyn another genuine smile which made her feel momentarily disconcerted.

'And Zac is just flying in from Zurich,' she said, her cheeks growing pink with pleasure. 'Where it appears that my husband has bought yet another hotel.'

It was only then that Tamsyn made the connection and she wondered how she could have been so dense. Emma was married to Zac Constantinides—the billionaire owner of the Granchester group of luxury hotels and Zac was Xan's *cousin*? Why hadn't Hannah reminded her of that? As the lift zoomed them back down to the hotel foyer, she wondered why she hadn't made the link herself, when it wasn't exactly the most common surname in the world. Probably because her mind and her body had been so full of new and conflicting emotions. And they still were. Surreptitiously, she touched her tongue to lips which were as dry as washing hung out in the sun, achingly aware that she was far from immune to the statuesque man who walked beside her.

They were shown into Garden Room, which overlooked an outdoor space which was surprisingly big, given its central London location. A discreet notice on the wall informed customers that the gardens had recently won a top horticultural award and although it was dark outside, cleverly placed lighting illuminated the tall shrubs and rare trees. As the maître d' showed them to what was obviously the best table—tucked away in a corner but with a birds-eye view of the floodlit gardens—Tamsyn became aware of people watching them. Or rather, they were watching Xan.

Did he realise that, or was his sense of self-worth so strong that he didn't notice?

'So why have you brought me here?' she questioned as she sat down to face a gleam of silver and crystal, tightening her hands as she laid them down on the snowy linen tablecloth. 'And more importantly, why have I *let* you?'

He paused for a moment while the waiter handed them menus, a wry smile touching the edges of his lips. 'Because we have been lovers and because you're curious.'

She gave a defiant tilt of her chin. 'I don't usually let people move me around like I'm a chip on the gaming table.'

'I get that. Just as I don't usually rush in and mastermind a transformation scene for my dinner dates,' he added drily, flicking her a cool cobalt gaze. 'You look absolutely sensational in that dress, by the way.'

Stupidly, the compliment made her want to squirm with pleasure until Tamsyn reminded herself that she still didn't know why she was here. But he was right. She *was* curious.

'So what do you want to talk about?'

'Why don't we choose what we want to eat first, otherwise the waiter will keep hovering over us.' He glanced at the menu before fixing her with his dark blue gaze. 'Would you like me to order for you?'

Tamsyn glared. Did he think she was so poor and humble that she'd couldn't interpret the French menu? Didn't he realise she'd worked in more fancy restaurants than he'd probably had hot dinners? She was sorely tempted to tell him she'd changed her mind, when she spotted something being lit with blue flames on a nearby table. Something delicious enough to make her mouth water and once again she was reminded that it was ages since she'd eaten.

'I'll have the lobster thermidor and the green salad with vinaigrette on the side,' she said carelessly. 'And no wine—just sparkling water.'

She enjoyed his faint look of surprise as he slapped his own menu shut and handed it to the waiter. 'I'll have the same,' he said, leaning back in his chair to study her.

'So,' she said, when he appeared in no hurry to break the silence. 'I'm still waiting for some sort of explanation. I mean, you've been content to ignore me for weeks and then you just turn up out of the blue and bring me here with the offer of some mystery proposition. What is it, Xan? Do you happen to own a café with an opening for a waitress who urgently needs a job?'

Xan realised that he was going to have to exercise great care in his choice of words because Tamsyn Wilson was both volatile and unpredictable. In a way she was the worst possible candidate for what he had in mind, but ironically it was her very unsuitability which made her the ideal candidate.

'You're in a bit of a fix right now aren't you, Tamsyn?' he questioned softly.

Her emerald eyes narrowed suspiciously. 'How do you know that?'

He shrugged. 'Call it intuition or call it observation. You seem to switch jobs quite frequently and being fired doesn't seem to freak you out as much as it would some people.' His gaze stayed fixed on her face. 'And I noticed you had a hole in your coat.'

She blushed and seemed to hesitate. As if wondering whether or not to brazen things out and keep pretending that, apart from urgently needing a job—everything else was okay. But the strain around her eyes told him that her plight was chronic and maybe she realised that, because some of her defiance seemed to ebb away as she lifted her shoulders in a shrug which didn't quite come off.

'I've known better times,' she admitted.

'But your sister has just married one of the wealthiest men in the world,' he probed. 'Surely she can come to your rescue if you're in need of money.'

For the first time he saw emotion on her face. Real emotion. Was it pride or distress which made her lips tremble like that? 'I'm not going to ask Hannah for help,' she said fiercely. 'She's helped me too often in the past and it's about time I stood on my own two feet.'

Xan nodded, realising that her misplaced pride was playing right into his hands. 'Then I think I can help you,' he said quietly. 'Or rather, I think we can help each other.'

She had recovered from her brief spell of vulnerability and that familiar challenge was back in her eyes. 'Me, help the powerful Xan Constantinides? Gosh. I can't imagine how I would do that.'

Xan paused for a moment because even though they meant nothing, the words he was about to say still had the power to make him tense. He'd had a blueprint for his life and up until now it had all gone according to plan, for he had micro-managed and controlled every part of it. It was how he had won a straight scholarship to Harvard from a humble village school and made a fortune in the property market, soon after graduating. He'd thought of matrimony to Sofia as just another stage in his game plan, but suddenly all that had changed. Suddenly he could understand why they called it wed*lock*. His eyes didn't leave Tamsyn's face.

'By marrying me,' he said.

CHAPTER SEVEN

XAN HAD NEVER seen anyone look so startled. Across the restaurant table, he watched Tamsyn's lips open and the pink tip of her tongue reminded him of the erotic pathways it had traced over his sweat-sheened skin. He shifted his weight a little and swallowed, because Tamsyn Wilson had given him more orgasms in a few short hours than any other woman—so many he'd lost count, and a man never forgot something like that.

The hardness in his groin increased, because didn't his current dilemma provide him with the perfect opportunity to feast on her delectable body once more? He hadn't pursued the affair not just because she was Kulal's new sister-in-law but because she had an inner wildness which made him uneasy—a wildness he had responded to in a way he didn't quite trust. Because something about her fire and her spirit had made him ignore his instinct to take her to bed in the first place. And ignoring his instincts had made him feel as if control was slipping away from him, which he didn't like. He didn't like it at all.

'Did you really just ask me to marry you?' she was saying, her green eyes unnaturally bright in the flicker of the candlelight.

'You want me to repeat it for you?' he drawled.

He was curious to see what her reaction would be, because that would colour his future behaviour towards her. If she looked as if he was about to present her with the moon on a platter and make her every dream come true, then he would have to be wary. But if, as he suspected—she cared as little for him as he did for her—there was no reason why they couldn't both enjoy what he had in mind.

But there was no sign of longing or triumph on her freckled face. Her green eyes were as suspicious as they'd been before. And Xan couldn't deny a brief kick of incredulity, for he was used to women making no secret of their adoration for him.

'Is this some kind of bad joke?' she was demanding. 'Have you had a bet with someone to see how much of a sucker I can be?'

He shook his head. 'I have often been described as difficult, but I am never knowingly cruel.'

There was a trace of uncertainty in her demeanour now. He could see her computing his words and failing to make sense of them.

She waited until the waiter had deposited their food in front of them before raising her eyebrows. 'So, why? I mean, why do you want to marry *me*? Did it take you all this time to realise that you can't possibly live without me and the only way to guarantee having me for the rest of your life is to slip a wedding ring on my finger?'

He stiffened before detecting sarcasm. 'Hardly,' he said.

She picked up her fork and hungrily began to eat. 'So why?'

Xan sucked in a long breath. Explanations he found

difficult. Almost as difficult as intimacy. It was in his nature to keep his thoughts and feelings to himself—or maybe that was just the way he'd been raised. His mother had been indifferent towards him and his father had been too busy trying to claw back his land and his heritage, to have any time for his only son. Either way, Xan had never let anyone close enough to worry about whether or not he trusted them. Yet to some extent he was going to *have* to trust Tamsyn Wilson if she agreed to his plan. And wouldn't that give her power over him? He swallowed, recognising that if he didn't want her abusing that power, he was going to have to reward her very handsomely.

'How much do you know about me?' he demanded.

She dabbed at her lips but the large linen napkin failed to hide her smile. 'You think I was so obsessed after our night in Zahristan that I hunted around to find out everything I could?'

'I don't know.' He sent her a look of challenge. 'Did you?'

'Funnily enough, no. I've had enough experience of lost causes to know when to quit. I certainly didn't waste any time mooning over someone who couldn't wait to get away from me. What do I know about you? Let me see.' She began to tap each finger, as if counting off the facts. 'Basically, you're loaded—my friend Ellie told me you were born mega-rich, though I think I could have worked that out for myself judging by your fancy suits and your swagger. My sister mentioned you were a hugely successful businessman—oh, and you're arrogant. I didn't need anyone to tell me that since that's a quality you seem to have in abundance.'

An unexpected smile touched the edges of Xan's lips. Clearly he wasn't going to have to worry about Tamsyn Wilson putting him on a pedestal!

'Anything else?' he questioned sardonically.

She shrugged. 'You don't seem as if you like me very much and yet now you're asking me to marry you?' She shook her red curls and scooped up another forkful of lobster. 'Forgive me if I sound confused— it's because I am.'

Discreetly, Xan gestured to the Sommelier, who returned moments later bearing a dusty bottle. A dark red liquid was dispensed into his glass and when Tamsyn shook her head in reply to the silent question in his eyes, he took a sip of the wine before continuing.

'There are only two things you need to know about me, Tamsyn,' he said. 'The first is that I believe there is no problem on this earth you can't buy your way out of, and the second is that there is a woman in Greece to whom I have been unofficially betrothed for many years.' He paused. 'Except I've realised that I cannot go through with it. I cannot marry her.'

He saw her eyes darken in distress. Saw the brief stabbing of her teeth into her lower lip before she displayed her more habitual air of nonchalance. 'Then don't. Just tell her. Dump her as comprehensively as you dumped me. She might be a bit upset but I should think one day she'll be grateful she isn't stuck with a misogynist like you for a lifetime. What's the problem, Xan? Has she found out you were sleeping with me—and maybe others—behind her back? Has she gone on the warpath in the way that only a jealous woman can?'

Angrily, Xan slammed his glass down on the table.

'Just for the record, I haven't had sex with anyone since the night I spent with you and I certainly haven't had sex with Sofia,' he growled. 'It's not that kind of relationship.'

At this, she put her fork down and the look she gave him was cynical. 'Let me guess,' she said tiredly. 'You play around and have your fun with women like me, is that right? And in the meantime there's a pure young virgin back home in Greece, just waiting for you? The age-old double standard of which so many men are guilty?'

Once again her perception startled him and she must have read the confirmation in his face because he could see her pushing her chair back as if preparing to walk out.

'You're disgusting!' she flared.

'Don't go,' he said urgently as he leant across the table towards her. 'Hear me out first. Please, Tamsyn.'

His words seemed to startle her but not nearly as much as they startled him because making pleas wasn't something he did very often. Had he thought she would be instantly malleable? So impressed by this introduction to a very different and glamorous kind of world, that she would leap at whatever he asked of her? Yes, he probably had thought exactly that. His lips flattened. How wrong he had been.

'What's there to hear?' she demanded.

'You said I was born wealthy but that certainly wasn't the case.'

'You mean you were born poor?' she questioned disbelievingly.

'Not poor but something in between. What is it they say? Asset rich, cash poor.' He met the question in her eyes and shrugged. 'My father inherited an island, a very beautiful island, called Prassakri. He was born there. Grew up there. Generations of his family lived and died there.' His voice tailed off as he recalled the story of how fortunes could wax, then wane without warning. 'Once many people inhabited that place, with enough work for all but gradually the work dried up and the young men began to leave, my father among them. Fortunately he had enough money to buy agricultural land on the mainland in Thessaly and for a while he was successful. But then came the drought, the worst drought the region had ever seen...'

His paused for a moment and she sat forward, genuine interest lighting up her freckled face. 'Go on,' she urged.

He grimaced. 'My father lost everything. And more. What the drought and resultant fires didn't take, bad investments soon took care of the rest. From being affluent, suddenly there wasn't enough food on the table. My mother took it badly.'

'How badly?' she questioned, her eyes narrowing.

'Badly enough.' He shut down her question sharply. Because he'd never talked about this with anyone. There hadn't really been the need to resurrect the pain and the discontent. Until now. 'The atmosphere of blame and recrimination in the house was unbearable,' he remembered suddenly, as he recalled walking into the house and seeing his mother's cold face and icy demeanour. 'My father was forced to sell the island to a neighbour and although it broke his heart to do so, he vowed that one day he would buy it back, because the bones of his ancestors are buried on that island and that means a great deal to a Greek.'

He took another mouthful of wine. 'Soon after that, land prices began rocketing and the purchase of Greek islands became beyond of the reach of most people. I could see my father's increasing powerlessness as he sensed the opportunity to buy back Prassakri slipping away from him. But his neighbour had a daughter—an only daughter—who just happened to be very beautiful. And I had just won a scholarship to an American college. It was a pretty big deal at the time and I was seen as someone who would one day make good. And that was when the neighbour made my father the offer.'

'What offer?' she breathed, her green eyes huge, her expression rapt.

'That if I were to marry Sofia, then he would allow my father to buy back the island at the original price.'

'And you agreed?' she breathed.

The facts when recounted now sounded like an extreme reaction but Xan recalled vividly that the offer had made perfect sense at the time. Hadn't he agreed in an attempt to bring about some sort of peace to his damaged family? To stop his mother haranguing his father with her bitter lament? *I didn't marry you in order to end up a pauper.*

'I was nineteen,' he said harshly. 'And it didn't seem real at the time. Sofia was a sweet young girl who would make any man a good wife, and if it meant the end to my father's heartache, then why wouldn't I agree? With one stroke I could restore the pride which was so important to him and maybe stop my mother from withdrawing more and more.'

'Yes, I know—but even so.' Sitting back in her chair with her hair looking like living flame in the candlelight, she threw him a perplexed look. 'It seems very extreme.'

'To be honest, I thought that Sofia would back out of the offer before I did,' he said, he said with a shrug. 'That she would fall in love and want to marry someone else.'

'But that didn't happen?'

'No.' He shook his head. 'It didn't happen. I tried to convince myself that arranged marriages work in many countries. That we share a common language and upbringing. And as time went on I found it a useful deterrent to the ambitions of other women, knowing I had an arranged marriage bubbling quietly away in the background and therefore was not in a position to offer them anything.'

'But you're a modern Greek! This sounds positively archaic.'

'I am not so modern as I might appear on the surface, Tamsyn.' His voice grew silky as he corrected her. 'At heart I have many values which some might consider old-fashioned.'

At this she screwed up her face, but not before he had seen the brief shiver rippling over her skin. Was she remembering how it had been between them in bed that night? When he'd experienced an almost *primitive* pleasure as he had broken through the tight barrier of her hymen and given an exultant shout of joy? No, he had been anything but modern that night.

'And what about love?' she challenged. 'Isn't that supposed to lie at the foundation of every marriage?'

His laugh was bitter but at least now he was on familiar territory. 'Not for me, Tamsyn. Only fools buy into romantic love.'

For the first time since they'd started this extraordinary conversation Tamsyn experienced a moment of real connection as she recognised a sentiment which was all too familiar. She thought about her feckless mother and the way she'd hocked up with all those different men. Hadn't that been why she and Hannah had been left abandoned and taken in by a pair of dysfunctional foster parents—because their mother had fallen *in love* for the umpteenth time? 'Well, that's one thing we do have in common,' she said. 'Since I feel exactly the same.'

He gave a cynical laugh. 'You actually say that like you mean it.'

'Why, do people normally say things just to please you?'

'Something like that,' he agreed.

Tamsyn wondered what it must be like if everyone was tiptoeing around you all the time. Was that what made him so sure of himself? 'So what's the problem?' she questioned. 'It sounds like the perfect solution. You've played the field and now you're settling down. A practical union between two people who know exactly where the boundaries lie.'

'And that's exactly what I thought—until the theory became reality and I realised there was no way I could marry Sofia.' He met the question in her green eyes. ' Oh, she's still a nice enough woman, but she is not my type Most of all, I do not desire her.' His voice hardened. 'And there can be no marriage without desire.' There was a long pause. 'Which is where you come in,' he added, breaking into her unsettled contemplation.

She narrowed her eyes. 'How?'

'I don't want to hurt Sofia or tarnish her reputation by telling her I don't want her. If I do that there's no way her father will sell back the island, even if I offer him double what it's worth by today's values.' Cobalt eyes bored into her. 'But an acceptable way of breaking off the engagement is to explain that I've fallen in love with someone else and am planning to marry her instead. Which will allow Sofia the chance to walk away with her pride intact.'

'You mean a fake marriage?' Tamsyn frowned. 'Like fake news?'

'A temporary marriage,' he amended drily. 'With a very generous divorce settlement at the end of it. Sofia gets a dignified let-out clause. I get to buy the island and you end up with a hefty pay-out. This could make you a very wealthy woman, Tamsyn. You could have the kind of lifestyle most people only dream of.'

Tamsyn stared at him, trying not to be swayed by the thought of all that money—but for someone who'd always lived hand-to-mouth, that was easier said than done. She thought about not having to watch every single penny. About being able to buy clothes which didn't come from the local market, or thrift store. She thought about having food in the fridge which wasn't past its sell-by date. Being able to take buses instead of walking all the time. Yes, it was tempting—but not tempting enough. Didn't Xan's arrogant certainty that there was no problem money couldn't solve make her want to reject his offer? Because she wasn't some *commodity*. She shook her curls. 'Go and ask someone else,' she said coldly. 'There must be loads more suitable candidates who would happily masquerade as your wife.'

'Oh, there are,' he agreed benignly. 'But that's the whole point. You are so eminently *unsuitable* that everyone will believe it's true love.'

His words hurt. Of course they did. Tamsyn might have always thought of herself as someone who didn't conform. Who swam against the tide. But considering yourself a bit of a rebel was very different to the man who'd been your first lover, saying you were the most unsuitable person he could think of to marry. Her heart clenched with pain and this time she really *did* want to get up from that pristine white table. In a parallel universe—she might have upended it, letting the crystal and the silver cutlery cascade to the floor in a satisfying cacophony of sound. But she'd tried that kind of approach with him once before and all it had done was made her look stupid.

And something was keeping her rooted to her seat. She tried telling herself she should wait to see how much he was offering in return for accepting his extraordinary proposal, but deep down Tamsyn knew it was more than that. He was right. She *was* curious.

'So why didn't you fancy her?' she questioned, like someone determined to rub salt into an already raw wound. As if by hurting herself, it meant nobody else would be able to. 'If she's so beautiful?"

Xan stared at his lobster which had already congealed on his plate. There was no need to explain that somehow, Tamsyn Wilson made every other woman look almost *tame* in comparison. That he hadn't been able to shift the stubborn memory of how her skin had tasted or how it had felt to have her legs wrapped around his thrusting hips. Why flatter her with the knowledge that she was the fire which made every other woman seem like a mere flicker? He swallowed. That kind of information was irrelevant.

'Chemistry is intangible,' he said roughly. 'It's not like a shopping list you just tick off as you go along.'

For the first time during the entire conversation, she smiled. 'You do a lot of shopping do you Xan?' she questioned. 'Somehow I can't really imagine you pushing a trolley round the supermarket,. I've certainly never see anyone like you when I'm stacking the shelves.'

Xan was unable to stop the brief curving of his lips in response. 'I buy cars and planes and works of art. The purchase of food I leave to my housekeeper. But you're trying to change the subject, Tamsyn. Is that because you find my suggestion unpalatable?' he said softly.

Tamsyn shrugged. She wasn't sure *how* she felt. About anything. Something told her to walk away while she still could, but she couldn't deny that the delicious food had lulled her into a state of sluggishness. And wasn't Xan's powerful presence only adding to her languor? Wasn't she stupidly reluctant to turn her back and never see him again? 'It's a crazy idea,' she said weakly.

He leaned forward as if sensing a window of opportunity and suddenly she could see why he was such a successful businessman.

'Imagine no longer having to work unless you wanted to. You could go back to school—you are an intelligent woman,' he said, his Greek accent dipping into a sultry caress. 'Imagine being able to live somewhere which isn't a…'

Tamsyn's shoulders stiffened as tactfully, his words faded away. 'Isn't a *what*?'

'It doesn't matter,' he said.

Somehow his careful diplomacy was more insulting than if he'd come right out and told her she lived in a slum. 'Of course it does! It matters to me. How the hell do you know where I live anyway?'

He gave her an odd kind of look. 'I had you checked out, of course.'

'You had me checked out,' she repeated slowly. 'By who?'

'There are people on my payroll who can find out almost anything. How else do you think I knew where you worked, Tamsyn?'

'I just assumed… I thought you might have asked the Sheikh.'

'No.' He shook his dark head. 'Kulal and Hannah know nothing about this.'

It was the mention of her sister's name which startled Tamsyn out of her lazy stupor. She had been about to tell Xan exactly what he could do with his offer—without letting him know how much he'd managed to hurt her. She would have told him that she mightn't have a job right now, but she would find one soon enough. She always did. Because one of the advantages of casual labour meant there were always vacancies for women like her. Women who had slipped through the net at school and at home. Who'd never had the comfort of regular meals or someone gently nagging at them to do their homework. She would get by because although she might not have any formal qualifications to her name, she was a graduate from the School of Survival. You didn't sleep in a room with winter frost inside the windows listening to sounds of arguments bouncing off the thin walls next door, without developing a tough exterior.

But what about Hannah? Her sister was in an entirely different situation. She might now be the wife of the world's richest men but that didn't necessarily mean she was safe. When she'd been in Zahristan for the wedding, Tamsyn had sensed all was not well in the new marriage. How could it be—when it had taken place between a powerful sheikh and someone as humble as Hannah? They had married because Hannah had been pregnant with the Sheikh's baby—but what if Kulal had only married her sister to get some kind of legal hold over his offspring? The Sheikh had all the power now that he had married her, didn't he? While Hannah had none. Not really. She might be the new Queen of a powerful desert region but she couldn't even speak the language of her adopted home.

Tamsyn folded up her napkin and placed it neatly on the table beside her empty plate. What if she agreed to Xan's crazy proposal, but on *her* terms? What if she demanded a whole load of money—more even than he'd probably contemplated giving her? Enough to bail out her sister, should the need ever arise. Wouldn't it be beyond fabulous to have enough cash to buy Hannah and her baby airline tickets out of Zahristan, if marriage to Kulal should prove intolerable? To give her a wad of that same cash to purchase a bolthole somewhere? Wouldn't it *mean* something to be able to do that—especially after everything her sister had done for her when they'd been growing up? To redress the balance a little. Even though...

Tamsyn swallowed down the suddenly acrid taste in her mouth.

Even though Hannah had been the reason Tamsyn had never met her father and it had taken her a long time to forgive her for that...

She looked up to find Xan watching her closely, the way she imagined a policeman might scrutinise a suspect from behind a piece of two-way glass. Well, he certainly wouldn't be able to read very much from *her* expression! Hadn't she spent all her formative years hiding her emotions behind the blasé mask she presented to the world?

'How long would this marriage last?'

'Not long. Three months should suffice. Any less than that and it will look like a stunt.'

She nodded. 'And how much money are you prepared to offer me?'

She saw him flinch—but that didn't surprise her either. Rich people never wanted to talk about money. They thought it was vulgar. Beneath them. Had Xan forgotten was it like to be poor, she wondered? Was that something else he'd blocked from his mind—like an agreement made by a teenage boy to marry a woman so his father could claw back an important piece of land?

'How much did you have in mind?' he questioned.

Her birth father had taught her everything she needed to know about desertion and rejection while her foster father's life lessons had been about infidelity and gambling. No wonder she distrusted men so much. But some of those lessons had been useful. She'd overheard enough bluster around card games to realise that you had to start high and be prepared to be knocked down whenever you were bargaining for something. So she mentioned an outrageous sum of money, prepared for yet slightly shamed by the brief look of contempt which hardened Xan's cobalt eyes. But it was gone almost immediately, because he nodded his head.

'Okay,' he said.

She blinked in disbelief. 'Just like that?'

He shrugged. 'You clearly want it. I can afford it. And obviously, the more I am prepared to pay—the more I get out of our brief union.'

The silky inference behind his drawled words made Tamsyn's stomach clench with anger. And something else. Something far more potent than anger. Because at times during his story she had wanted to reach out to him. To comfort him? Or to kiss him? Or both. Maybe both. Especially when his face had grown hard and hurt when he'd mentioned his mother. She could feel her breasts pushing against the fine wool of the cashmere dress as she directed him a heated look, forcing herself to be bold enough to ask the question. 'You think I'm going to have *sex* with you?'

'That's a pretty naive question, Tamsyn,' he answered softly. 'Why wouldn't I? We've had sex before and it was good. Very, very good.' He raised his eyebrows. 'And isn't it a very necessary part of the marriage contract?

There was a pause during which Tamsyn steeled herself against the shocking beauty of his face and her own even more shocking reaction to him...the heat of excitement in her blood and the soft throb of hunger between her legs. But somehow, using the kind of resilience which every abandoned child needed in order to survive, she managed to present to him a face devoid of expression. 'Not in this case, because it's only make-believe,' she said coolly. 'I'll marry you because I want your money. But it's nothing but a business arrangement and there's no way I'm being intimate with you again, Xan. Because it wouldn't be right. Not after everything that's happened.'

CHAPTER EIGHT

SOMEHOW THE FLOWERS woven into her hair stayed in place, even though the sea breeze was whipping wildly all around her. Tamsyn guessed that was one of the benefits of marrying a billionaire—that he could afford to pay a top hairdresser to tame his prospective wife's unruly curls into an elaborate style which had miraculously stayed put all day. She clutched the railings of Xan's luxury yacht as it skimmed through the sapphire waters, trying to get her head around the fact that she was now the Greek tycoon's wife, and that the shiny golden ring which glinted on her finger was for real.

Well, as real as a fake wedding would allow.

Determined not to let herself be led like a lamb to the slaughter on her wedding day, she'd stated her terms before the ceremony, insisting she didn't want a big fuss—opting instead for something low-key and pared down. She thought it would have felt *cheap* to put on a big public show which meant nothing, and there was no way she could have made hollow vows in a place of worship. Most important of all, she didn't want Hannah hearing about the marriage until it was over, just in case she decided to do something dramatic like arriving in a flurry of royal pomp to try and talk her out of it.

But keeping their nuptials quiet seemed to have appealed to Xan as well and in a quiet moment he'd admitted that he had no stomach for weddings in general and his own in particular.

'The details will be posted in the local town hall which is a requirement by law,' he said. 'But since the mayor is a friend, our privacy will be respected and there's no way word will get out to the press. At least, not until I am ready to issue a statement.' A hard glimmer of a smile had followed. 'And it adds a little passionate *authenticity* to our whirlwind romance if we keep it all very hush-hush don't you think, *agape mou*?

What Tamsyn thought wasn't really here nor there. It bothered her that Xan seemed to be almost *relishing* the clandestine nature of the wedding, until she forced herself to remember that most men enjoyed secrecy. This was nothing but an elaborate game to Xan, she reminded herself, and since they weren't planning to be married for very long, what was the point in objecting?

'We will have a big party straight after the honeymoon,' Xan had informed her the day after she'd accepted his proposal, when he had turned up unexpectedly at her tiny bedsit, his lips curving with distaste as he looked around, before announcing that from then on she would be staying at the Granchester until the wedding. 'A big, lavish party to which we will invite family and close friends, and announce that we are man and wife.'

'And Sofia?' Tamsyn's voice had asked, wondering how the Greek woman who had been Xan's bride intended would take the sudden news. 'When are you planning to tell her?'

'I will phone her after the ceremony, once I've spoken to my father.'

Something about the obvious omission made her tentatively ask the question. 'And what about…your mother?'

She had never seen his face so expressionless. As if it had been wiped clean of all feeling—his features looking as if they had been hewn from some dark and impenetrable marble. 'My mother died a decade ago.'

'Oh, Xan, I'm sorry.'

It had been an instinctive condolence on her part but he hadn't wanted it, cutting short the conversation with a cool determination she had come to recognise as Xan's way of doing things. And in a way she could understand his reluctance to talk. She didn't want to him delving into *her* past, did she? Didn't want him probing her own areas of painful memory. Why rake all that up, when this was a relationship which was never intended to last?

'But do you think Sofia will be upset?' she had persisted. 'The last thing I want is to cause another woman pain.'

His mouth had hardened. 'Let's hope not. Maybe she will have realised that she's better off without a man like me,' he'd added, his voice growing harsh. 'A man who cannot give her the love she deserves.'

Recalling those words, it was difficult for Tamsyn not to conclude that he considered her somehow unworthy of those things. In Xan's mind she was greedy and acquisitive. He thought of her as a gold-digger, just like her sister—she knew that. And although it wasn't necessary for him to have a high opinion of her, she couldn't deny it hurt that he thought so little of her.

They had married in a tiny ceremony outside Athens earlier that day—without fuss or fanfare, just two anonymous witnesses plucked from the street and a single photographer, who had captured the event for posterity. It was the first time she'd seen Xan smile all day.

'It will be no hardship to lose the obnoxious tag of "Greece's most eligible bachelor",' he had drawled, those thick, dark lashes shuttering the cobalt brilliance of his eyes. 'At least in future I might just be left alone to get on with my life and to live it as I please.'

His words had been arrogant enough to make Tamsyn bristle, but she'd bitten back her sarcastic response, deciding that having a stand-up fight right before the ceremony might not be the best way of portraying marital harmony. Instead, she'd concentrated on her appearance, determined to play her own part with aplomb. She'd chosen an extremely short white wedding dress in diaphanous layers of silk-chiffon which came to mid-thigh and defined the shape of her legs beneath. It was pretty and delicate as well as being slightly daring, but that was exactly what she wanted. She wanted people to look at her and tut. To remark that she really *was* an outrageous choice of bride for the Greek tycoon because that would pave the way for their speedy divorce.

What she hadn't banked on was Xan's reaction when he saw her walking towards him clutching a scented bunch of white flowers. He had looked her up and down as if he couldn't quite believe what he was seeing, his gaze lingering on her bare legs and a little muscle flickering at his temple. And when she'd enquired—a little anxiously—if the short dress was emphasising the freckles on her thighs, he had given her an odd kind of smile before shaking his head and guiding her towards the car waiting to take them to Piraeus.

'Not at all, *agape mou*.' His denial had been husky and the little muscle had still been flickering at his temple. 'Not at all.'

And now she and her new husband were skimming over the sapphire sea towards the Peloponnese peninsula, because Xan had told her the best way to see his home for the first time was from the water. Almost as if was a *real* honeymoon and he was trying to impress her!

She'd never been on a yacht before—just ferries—most memorably a day-trip to Calais when she'd been just seventeen. But Xan's sleek craft was worlds away from the lumbering ferry which had moved through the water with all the grace of a giant tractor. This boat gleamed silvery-white in the spring sunshine. It drew the eye of every passing yacht—especially with Xan at the helm. He had swapped his dark wedding suit for a pair of faded denims and a white T-shirt which emphasised the contrasting gleam of his olive skin. The muscles in his arms bunched as he did impressive-looking things to the billowing sails and his raven-dark hair rippled in the Aegean breeze. With an effort, Tamsyn tried to concentrate on the horizon, trying to prevent her gaze from sliding to his powerful body as he tugged on a rope—as she wondered how difficult it was going to be to resist him during the fortnight's honeymoon which lay ahead.

'Tamsyn! Look over there.'

Over the white noise whoosh of the sea, Xan's voice broke into her thoughts and Tamsyn glanced up to follow the direction of his gaze. She hadn't really thought about what she might find at the end of her journey but now her heart contracted with something like yearning as suddenly she understood the meaning of the word paradise.

Xan's home was situated on a strip of land surrounded on three sides by the sea, like a green finger dipping into pot of blue water. A large, elevated modern house glinted in the bright sunshine of the spring morning but there were other buildings occupying the sprawling estate too, which made her realise just how vast it was. Outside seating areas with wicker chairs and tables and a long veranda, festooned with bright flowers and green climbers. In the distance was the seductive glitter of a sapphire swimming pool which blended into the ocean beyond, and impossibly smooth, emerald lawns sloping down a private beach, where a curve of sugar-white sand tempted the eye. Tamsyn watched as Xan expertly brought the yacht skimming into the small harbour where two fishermen were waiting, greeting him affectionately as they helped him anchor the boat.

Still in her wedding heels, Tamsyn consented to being lifted onto the sand by her new husband, which she supposed only added to the supposed romance of their arrival. And despite trying to convince herself that the gesture was functional rather than emotional, that didn't stop her skin from shivering in response when he briefly held her in his powerful arms. Did her eyes darken or some other barely visible response communicate itself to him? Was that why there was a speculative narrowing of his eyes? Tamsyn stiffened. Just because she *felt* desire, didn't mean she was going to act on it, did it? Even if it *was* difficult to shake the memories of just how good it had been between them...

'Let's go up to the house,' he said, indicating a steep flight of stone steps, before casting a doubtful look at her towering white heels. 'Think you can manage to walk in those, or would you like me to carry you?'

'I think I can manage,' she said, seeing the answering smile which curved his lips.

'I thought you might say that,' he commented drily.

But by the time they reached the top of the steps with Tamsyn panting slightly, Xan caught hold of her hand, lacing his fingers in hers as they began to walk towards the lawn.

She shot him a questioning glance, hating the sudden thrill of her hand as it was enclosed in the warmth of his. 'Xan?' she said breathlessly.

'My housekeeper is watching from the house,' he said. 'And I know how disappointed she would be if she thought we were anything other than a pair of deliriously happy newlyweds.'

His housekeeper was watching.

Well, what had she expected? That he had been suddenly overcome with emotion? Tamsyn tried to pull away but he stayed her with the feather-light circling of his thumb and instead she found herself shivering in response. What was the *matter* with her? Was she so starved of physical affection that even a tiny stroke could reduce her to such a state of longing? Maybe she was. Or maybe gestures like that mimicked *real* closeness and made her realise with a sudden shock just what she'd never had. No mother to cuddle her. No father to bounce her on his knee. Nobody except Hannah who back then had only ever given her the occasional half-hearted hug, because it was kind of embarrassing to cuddle your kid sister.

So remember why you're here, she told herself fiercely. Remember why you're doing this. Not for love, or scraps of affection, but for *money*. Money for Hannah—the only person who'd ever really been there for her.

But it was easy to forget reality when the house-keeper was standing in the doorway watching them approach, her face creased with pleasure as she clapped her gnarled hands together in delight. The greeting she gave Xan was a surprise—Tamsyn hadn't expected the tycoon to consent to being embraced so fervently by his elderly housekeeper. But neither was she prepared for the crushing embrace to which *she* was subjected afterwards and for a moment she stood, stiff as a board before gradually relaxing into the woman's cushioned flesh. And wasn't she secretly glad of that brief opportunity to compose herself and the chance to blink away the tears which had inexplicably sprung to her eyes.

'Tamsyn, this is Manalena,' Xan was saying as the woman relinquished her hold at last. 'Who has been with the family for a very long time.'

'*Kalispera!*' beamed Manalena, mimicking a rocking movement with her arms. 'I have known Kyrios Xan since he was a baby.'

It was difficult to imagine this towering man as a baby, thought Tamsyn. To picture him small and helpless and vulnerable. 'And was he a good baby?' she asked, with a smile.

Manalena gave a shake of her greying head. 'He never sleep and when he was a little boy, he never sit still. He is still like that now, and I am very happy he find a wife at last.'

Tamsyn remembered Xan telling her that his engagement to Sofia had been a private matter and for that she was grateful. Imagine if his staff regarded her as some kind of usurper and resented her, making her sense of isolation even more pronounced. She wondered how the housekeeper would feel if she knew the truth behind their whirlwind wedding and that Tamsyn was not the genuine and loving bride she must have hoped for. A flicker of discomfort washed over her as she glanced up at Xan while Manalena spoke to him in a torrent of rapid and babbled Greek.

'Manalena has just been explaining that a special wedding breakfast has been prepared for us,' he translated. 'She is also complaining that this morning a member of my staff arrived from Athens and is getting under her feet.'

As if on cue, a sleek brunette emerged from the house, talking excitedly into a cellphone, before quickly terminating the call. Slim and sophisticated, it was impossible to know exactly how old she was, though Tamsyn would have guessed mid to late thirties. Shiny shoulder-length hair swung in a raven arc around her chin and her linen trousers and pristine cream blouse made her appear the very definition of cool. In her too-short wedding dress with the flowers beginning to wilt in her windswept curls, Tamsyn felt inferior in comparison, even though the woman was smiling at her in a friendly manner.

'Hello! You must be Tamsyn,' she said, her perfect English tinged with a fetching Greek accent. 'I'm Elena and I'm very pleased to meet you and to offer my congratulations.'

'Elena is my personal assistant from the Athens office,' explained Xan. 'She's been overseeing all the wedding party preparations.'

'I hope everything will be to your satisfaction,' said Elena quickly. 'Xan gave me *carte blanche* to make decisions about food and drink and decorations, so I did. I would have communicated with you directly except—'

'I told Elena you were busy winding up your life in England,' said Xan, meeting Tamsyn's eyes with a bland look.

Tamsyn forced a smile because what could she say? That packing up her few miserable possessions had taken about five minutes and she might have welcomed having a little input into her own wedding party, rather than sitting around in the unfamiliar luxury of the Granchester Hotel, wondering what on earth she had let herself in for. Xan had given her a credit card and told her to buy an entire new wardrobe, one befitting the wife of a Greek tycoon. And although Tamsyn had half-heartedly done as he'd asked, she'd bought only what was strictly necessary, obsessively keeping all the receipts so that they could be included in a final tally when the divorce settlement came through.

Perhaps Xan had drafted Elena because he was afraid his new wife might prove incapable of choosing a sophisticated menu for their wedding party, despite holding her own that night they'd dined together at the Granchester. Or maybe he was worried she might let slip the true nature of their whirlwind romance—although he didn't seem to be doing anything to bolster the false fairytale himself. He wasn't exactly acting like a man who'd been swept away by passion, was he? She doubted whether that brief hand-holding exhibition would have convinced his housekeeper—or anyone else—that this marriage was for real.

'I'm very grateful for your help,' she told Elena brightly. 'For a start, I don't speak any Greek.'

'Well no, not *yet*,' said Elena with a friendly grin. 'But you will. Like your new husband, it isn't easy—but it's certainly possible to master.'

'I think you should kiss goodbye to your bonus, Elena,' said Xan mildly, propelling Tamsyn forward with the brief caress of his fingers. 'Come and meet the rest of the staff.'

The *rest* of the staff? Exactly how many people did he have working for him? Suddenly Tamsyn felt daunted by the line of workers who were waiting to meet her. Silently, she repeated their names before saying them out loud, terrified she would forget them before wondering why she was so anxious to please. There was Rhea the cook and pretty young Gia, who was in charge of the cleaning. A part-time driver named Panos, and Orestes the gardener, whose wife Karme helped Gia in the house when the need arose.

Tamsyn said hello to them all, using the few words of Greek she'd managed to learn before leaving England, but once again she felt faintly uneasy about deceiving these people who obviously adored her Greek husband and wanted the best for him.

Once again Manalena said something in Greek and Xan nodded, before glancing briefly at his watch.

'The meal is almost ready, but there are a couple of phone calls I need to make first,' he said. 'Manalena will show you where to freshen up and I'll meet you downstairs in the dining room in ten minutes.'

Feeling as if she'd been dismissed, Tamsyn followed the housekeeper up a sweeping staircase to the first floor, wondering how Xan was expecting to maintain the image of doting bridegroom if he couldn't even be bother to show her to the bathroom himself! Yet she couldn't deny a feeling of relief, that she would be spared the intimate reality of their shared marital space for at least a little while longer.

She walked down a wide and airy corridor, past walls covered with dramatic seascapes, until at last Manalena halted in front of a set of double doors. 'This is your room,' said Manalena, a note of pride creeping into her voice as she pushed open one of the doors.

Tamsyn walked into a room of breathtaking splendour with views right over the water, so that sunlight danced in an ever-moving lightshow over the pale walls. On the dressing table she could see the a pair of gold cufflinks set with sapphires which perfectly matched her new husband's eyes. Xan's room, she thought. And now hers, too. Her throat constricted. If it had belonged to anyone else she would have walked straight over to the window and feasted her eyes on the dark swell of the sea, but her attention was caught by something else. By the vast bed, on whose snowy covers someone had scattered pink rose petals—dozens of them—their scented splendour seeming to mock her.

Another reminder of a romance which wasn't real, she reminded herself, trying to erase the stupid sense of wistfulness which was clenching at her heart. Yet what could she do other than smile at the faithful housekeeper who stood anxiously in front of her, obviously awaiting her verdict on the honeymoon suite.

'It looks very beautiful, Manalena,' she said softly. '*Efkaristo.*'

Looking gratified, Manalena beamed and nodded. 'I wait for you outside.'

Alone at last, Tamsyn kicked off her high-heeled shoes and wiggled her newly liberated toes. And even though she could have happily thrown herself onto the bed and tried to blot out what was coming next, she freshened up in the lavish bathroom, helping herself from a selection of costly bath products which had obviously been acquired for the new bride. Pulling the wilting flowers from her hair, she raked a brush through her hair, gradually removing the tangles until it fell in a thick and vibrant curtain all the way down to her waist. She eyed the spindly wedding shoes doubtfully and decided against putting them back on. With a final tug at her short dress, she went back downstairs with Manalena, where Xan was waiting for her in the dining room.

And Tamsyn could do nothing about the overwhelming rush of desire which pulsed over her. It seemed incongruous to see the Greek tycoon standing there, still in his sailing clothes, his cobalt eyes darkening with unmistakable appreciation as he surveyed her. Her heart began to thunder as she realised that this powerful man was now her husband.

And she needed to keep it together. Not let desire

*weaken her. To remember that this was nothing but an
elaborate ruse. A business transaction, that was all.*

'You don't look much like a bridegroom,' she commented lightly, in a vain attempt to defuse the sudden
tension which seemed to have accompanied her into
the room.

His gaze raked over her, lingering on the filmy
white dress and focussing last on her bare feet whose
toenails were painted a shimmering iridescent silver.
'Whereas you look exactly like a bride, *agape mou*,'
he said unevenly. 'If a somewhat unconventional one.'

'Wasn't that the whole idea?' she questioned acidly.

Xan couldn't quite bring himself to answer, because
he wasn't sure *where* his head had been when he'd
asked Tamsyn Wilson to marry him. Had he thought
she would be easily manipulated? That her humble
status and the knowledge he was paying her a great
deal of money, would give him the upper hand? Yes,
he had. Guilty on all counts.

Pulling out a chair for her, he felt the silkiness of
her loose curls brushing tantalisingly against his hand
and his groin hardened. He hadn't believed her when
she'd told him there was to be no sex, but her distant
behaviour since they'd made their deal, had convinced
him that she'd meant every word she said. He'd tried
convincing himself that he wouldn't find it too much
of a problem—and that three months enforced celibacy was easily doable. What he had failed to take into
account was just how entrancing he would continue
to find her, or that her stubbornness would act as an
aching kind of aphrodisiac. His mouth hardened. He
should have picked a bride from the type of woman
with which he was familiar. The type who would jump

when he snapped his fingers. Who would do whatever he asked of them, and do it with gratitude and pleasure. Not some feisty woman who seemed determined to oppose him every step of the way.

He poured two glasses of vintage champagne and handed her one, his throat drying with lust as their eyes met over the rims of the fine crystal. Suddenly he wished he'd told Manalena that they would eat something light on the balcony of his bedroom, so that he could have had Tamsyn all to himself. To test just how strong her resolve was. Too late, he thought grimly, knowing how much trouble his cook would have gone to.

But his expression betrayed none of his disquiet as he raised his glass to hers. 'So. What shall we drink to, Tamsyn?' he questioned.

For a moment she looked uncertain—like a small creature who'd strayed too far from her natural habitat. She stared down at the fizzing wine before lifting her gaze and chinking her crystal glass against his.

'To money, of course,' she said defiantly. 'That's what this is all about, isn't it? Money and land.'

And all that flippancy was back—the defiant tilt of her chin just daring him to challenge her, when ironically—all it made him want to do was kiss her.

CHAPTER NINE

IT WAS THE longest meal she'd ever endured but Tamsyn was determined to spin out her wedding breakfast as long as she could. Because eating and drinking would delay the inevitable—and she was terrified of accompanying Xan upstairs, to that vast bed scattered with pink rose petals. Terrified that she would give into the demands of her traitorous body and fall hungrily into his arms. Because that was the last thing she needed.

Dutifully she picked at course after delicious course, trying to give every impression of enjoying the food which had been so carefully prepared by Rhea, the cook. The Greek salad topped with fragrant basil, still warm from the herb garden. The fish with delicious sauce, followed by *giovetsi*—a dish of lamb baked in a clay pot, served with green beans stewed with tomatoes. Rhea's final flourish was a traditional wedding dessert called *diples*, a sweet fried concoction covered in a great deal of honey and crushed walnuts. The honey kept sticking to the roof of her mouth and she really didn't need another morsel, but Tamsyn was determined to eat it.

And each course had an accompanying wine—fine wines in different colours. Tamsyn rarely drank but today she sipped a little, so that by the time the sweet wine was served with dessert, she felt better than she had in days. It was as if a tight knot at the base of her stomach had slowly begun to unfurl, allowing her to relax at last.

Staring across the table at Xan, she tried not be affected by his rugged masculine beauty, but that was easier said than done. His skin gleamed like gold in the sunlight and the close-fitting jeans and T-shirt gave him a deceptively laid-back air. At times she was in danger of forgetting that he was a billionaire control freak who was calling all the shots, because right now he looked like some rippling-fleshed fisherman who'd just wandered up to the house for a bit of lunch.

'So,' she said, finally admitting defeat and putting her dessert spoon down. 'Here we are. Mr and Mrs Constantinides. How weird is that?'

A glint of amusement entered the cobalt eyes. 'Pretty weird,' he admitted.

'Have you issued your statement to the press yet? Is that what the phone call was all about?'

'I have no intention of speaking to the press today, Tamsyn. I will respond to questions if and when necessary. I was speaking to my father.' There was a pause. 'And Sofia.'

Tamsyn felt her heart lurch. 'And?'

'Sofia took it better than I expected. She seemed more resigned than upset. Which is a good thing.'

'Like I said,' Tamsyn observed. 'She's probably secretly pleased not to have to spend a lifetime with you.'

'Thanks for the vote of confidence, sweetheart,' he said drily.

She wanted to tell him not to tease her like that,

just like she wanted to tell him not to look at her with that sexy glint of amusement in his eyes. Mainly because she liked it. She liked it way too much. It made her want to do what she had vowed she wasn't going to do—mainly to rush upstairs and get up close and personal with him. She cleared her throat. 'And your father?'

For the first time, his face showed a flicker of darkness. 'My father took the news less well. He was angry, which didn't surprise me, but his concerns were focussed more on his island inheritance than on the people involved. No change there.' His laugh was tinged with bitterness. 'He seems to think that Sofia's father might refuse to sell me the island now that I've jilted his daughter. I think it will depend on Sofia's reaction, but better that than breaking her heart,' he added harshly.

'And if he's right? If Sofia's father won't sell?'

'Oh, if Sofia is okay, he'll sell—don't you worry about that.'

'How can you be so sure?'

'Because Tamsyn, everyone has their price' He gave a cynical smile. 'Even you.'

It was a timely reminder of her new husband's cold-heartedness but Tamsyn forced herself not to react, instead fixing him with a look of interest. 'Is your father coming to the wedding party?'

'He said not, but I know his bluster of old and he'll be there—if only because the cream of Athenian and international society will be attending and he'd hate to miss out.'

'And in the meantime, we have a whole two week honeymoon to get through.' Tamsyn resisted the temptation to chew on her fingernails which had been varnished silver to match her toes. 'Wasn't that a rather unnecessary addition to this sham marriage?'

'I told you. We don't want to make it look like a stunt.' He leaned back in his chair to study her. 'And we can make this as easy or as difficult as we like.'

Tamsyn wondered if he was out of his mind. Didn't he realise that there was a constant battle raging inside her? That while her head was telling her not to have sex with her new husband—her body was urging her in the opposite direction. Did Xan know that every time she looked at him she wanted to touch him, even though to do so would be madness. Or that at night she was haunted by the memories of his hard body thrusting into hers and giving her pleasure, over and over again? Running her trembling fingertip round the edge of her crystal glass, she struggled to find a neutral topic. 'Manalena seems very sweet,' she said at last.

'She is.' He took a mouthful of wine, his expression mocking her.

'Why did she used to look after you? Did your mother go out to work?'

'No. But motherhood appealed to her about as much as being poor, and she didn't care who knew it. Including me, just for the record. She went to great pains to assure me that some women simply weren't maternal, and she was one of them.'

His words were terse and he spoke them as if they didn't matter but they told her a lot, mainly that his mother had been emotionally distant. Tamsyn nodded, wondering just how far she could push him—without stopping to ask herself why she wanted to. 'Do you think that's what made you so…'

'So what, Tamsyn?' he questioned sardonically as her words tailed off.

'So… I don't know.' She straightened her napkin so that it lay at a ninety-degree angle next to her place-setting, just as she would have done if she'd been at work. 'So anti-love and marriage…'

He shrugged. 'That's what the psychologists would say, I guess.'

'And was it bad?' she questioned suddenly, her heart going out to him despite telling herself that he didn't need her sympathy. 'Your childhood, I mean?'

'Bad enough. But I happened to like the independence which came about as a result of having a mother who was never there for me. The thought of having to answer to someone every hour of every day filled me with horror and still does.' His eyes were like dark blue ice. 'In future all my bios will say, *he was briefly married.* And you, *agape mou*, will have liberated me from the expectation which society heaps on every wealthy man, that he is not complete until he finds himself a suitable wife. You will have done me a big favour, Tamsyn.' His lips curved into a reflective smile. 'And that in itself is worth the money I'm paying you to wear my ring.'

His mocking words effectively terminated the conversation, but it left Tamsyn thinking that maybe they were more similar than she'd imagined, despite the great difference in their lifestyles.

'So what now?' she questioned, aware that they couldn't sit amid the debris of their wedding breakfast all day.

His eyes gleamed. 'Now that you've made lunch last as long as you possibly could?'

'I was hungry.'

'Of course you were, *agape mou*,' he agreed, silkily. 'Hungry enough to pick at your food with marked indifference and then to push it around your plate? But your face is pale and your eyes strained, so I suggest you retire to the bedroom and take an afternoon nap. It's been a long day.'

His words made sense because Tamsyn *was* tired. But the memory of that petal-strewn bed kept flickering into her mind and she knew she couldn't keep skirting round the issue. In London she'd told him there was to be no sex and he needed to realise she meant it. But she couldn't discuss the subject here—not with Manalena poking her beaming head around the door and asking if they'd like coffee.

Her husband declined the offer, his drawled response bringing an instant smile to Manalena's face as she remained in the doorway, watching them. And when Xan walked around the table and held out his hand towards Tamsyn, she found herself taking it. She told herself she was doing this for the housekeeper's benefit and maybe she was. But she couldn't deny that she was enjoying the sensation of Xan's strong fingers encircling hers, as he led her upstairs towards the master bedroom. Of course she was. Because in those few moments she felt safe. As if nothing could ever harm her so long as she was with this powerful and charismatic man.

And that was nothing but an illusion. She was nothing but a bought bride, to be disposed of as soon as possible.

She was shivering as he closed the bedroom door behind them, acutely aware of the intimacy of the enclosed space. She ran her fingertips over the wilting bouquet she'd placed on a nearby table and then, when there was no room left for prevarication, looked into his face. 'Where am I sleeping?'

He raised his eyebrows. 'Judging by the amount of petals which seem to have been offloaded onto the bed, I'd say right here.'

She shook her head, hating the sudden hot prickle of her breasts. 'I told you I didn't want any intimacy, Xan, so therefore it makes more sense for me to have my own bedroom.'

'And if I were to grant you your wish, that would bring into question the validity of our marriage,' he answered coolly. 'Which kind of defeats the whole purpose of you being here.'

'So we've got to share a bed?'

'It's a very large bed.'

'I can see that for myself. But it doesn't matter how big it is,' she snapped. 'I don't want…'

'What don't you want, Tamsyn?'

She stiffened as she heard the soft mockery in his voice. Was he going to make her spell it out? And if he was, so what? She was no longer the shrinking little virgin who had given herself to him one starry desert night, even if right now she felt like it. This man knew her like no other. He had kissed her lips and suckled her breasts. He had shown her how he liked to be touched and stroked and had then thrust deep inside her hungry body. He had seen her vulnerable in the midst of her orgasm. Had heard her stumble out his name in a choking cry as she tumbled over the edge. Surely that gave her the right to say what was on her mind. 'Sex,' she managed, her cheeks growing hot.

'It isn't obligatory to have sex with me.' He shrugged. 'I'm not planning to demand my conjugal rights, if that's what you're worried about. Like I said, it's a big bed.'

'And you think it's possible for us to lie side by side and, and...' Her voice tailed off, unable to articulate the confusion of her feelings which were compounded by the sheer depth of her inexperience. Did he guess that? Was that why the look he slanted her seemed almost *compassionate*?

'I think it's possible,' he said slowly. 'It won't be easy and it certainly won't be enjoyable, but in the end the decision is yours, Tamsyn. Yet all you have to do is say the word and we could have one hell of a honeymoon.'

Her cheeks grew even hotter. 'I don't know how you can be...so...*callous*.'

'And I don't know why you're making such a big deal out of it. You think every time a couple have sex, there has to be some great big emotion underlying it?' His cobalt gaze seared into her. 'Didn't it ever occur to you that sexual gratification is just one of life's fundamental pleasures, Tamsyn?'

Tamsyn was aware of a sudden emptiness. A disappointment. As if he'd just burst some invisible bubble. As if the stories women told themselves about happy-ever-after really *were* a myth. 'And that's all there is to it?' she asked, in a small flat voice.

He shrugged. 'It exists for the procreation of children, but that's not going to be an issue for us, is it?'

'No,' she agreed, unprepared for another unexpectedly painful clench of her heart. 'It's not going to be an issue.'

'Don't take it so personally,' he advised softly. 'Sex doesn't have to be about love.'

'I realise that. I may be relatively inexperienced, but I'm not stupid!' she declared. 'I'm not looking for love but if I was, you'd be right at the bottom of my wish-list, Xan Constantinides!'

Her words sounded genuine and Xan gave the ghost of a smile because she really was surprising. Up-close contact with his enormous wealth didn't seem to have blunted her determination to do things *her* way, nor to subdue her feisty nature. She was behaving like his equal and that was doing dangerous things to his libido. He was used to female subjugation and was finding the lack of it a powerful aphrodisiac. Lust pulsed through him, hot and potent. She was such a contradiction in so many ways. Tough and outspoken—and yet at times he was certain he'd detected a glimpse of frailty beneath her waspish exterior. And didn't that intrigue him? Make him wonder what had put it there?

He stared out of one of the windows where he could see Orestes tending to the violet blooms of an exotic flower and he thought about the fortnight ahead, realising that this fabricated honeymoon would drag like hell unless he could find something pleasurable to fill the time. And sex with his fiery new bride would certainly while away the hours in the most delicious way.

She hadn't moved from where she'd been standing and he reached out to touch his fingertip against her mouth, instantly feeling it tremble. He could see her throat constricting and her eyes briefly closing as if she was trying to fight her own desire. And that turned him on even more, because he wasn't used to women fighting their attraction to him. 'You still want me, Tamsyn,' he observed thickly. 'And it's the same for me. I want you so much that I'm aching just thinking about it.'

He could see the uncertainty flickering in the depths of her green eyes. 'Nobody's denying the desire, Xan. Doesn't mean we're going to do anything about it though.'

'Why not?'

'Because....' She moved away from him then, wriggling her shoulders restlessly as the little white wedding dress shimmied provocatively over her bare thighs. 'It seems wrong to have sex just for the sake of it.'

'Says who? Why does it bother you so much?'

She stared at him and suddenly her eyes were very bright. 'It doesn't matter.'

'Oh, but it does. I'm interested in why you're such a fundamentally old-fashioned young woman at heart.'

Tamsyn gave a careless shrug which didn't quite come off, because it was difficult to remain indifferent to her past when he was looking at her so piercingly.

'I didn't realise I was.'

'Psychologists usually say it something to do with your parents and your upbringing,' he said wryly. 'So let's start with that.'

This is what she'd been trying to avoid telling him. But what difference did it make if she told him about her mother? This part of her life wasn't the part she had buried in a deep, dark place which she never ventured near.

'I don't remember my birth mother, because I was just a baby when she gave me and Hannah up for adoption,' she said baldly. 'But nobody wanted to adopt us because we were too much of a handful. Or rather, I was. Apparently it's quite common for abandoned babies to grow into troublesome children.' She shrugged. 'That's why we put up with so much from our foster parents, despite all their failings.' She shrugged as she met the question in his eyes. 'There was a terrible atmosphere in the house, mainly because my foster father used the grocery money to fund his card games, or to buy dinner for one of his many mistresses. We were terrified that if we complained we'd get split up. And neither Hannah or I could bear the thought of that.'

There was a silence during which she thought he was about to let it go. And didn't she *want* him to let it go?

'So what do you know about your birth mother, Tamsyn,' he prompted softly.

Tamsyn swallowed. If she told him he would judge her and she didn't want to be judged. Because that's what the girls at school had done, once they found out about her mum. They'd picked on her and bullied her and the strong skin she'd grown had been as a direct result of that. But talking about it would reinforce the certainty that there could never be any kind of future between her and Xan. And it might stop him from probing further—keeping him away from the stuff which was *really* unpalatable.

She shrugged. 'From what I understand, she was pretty liberal with her body. She liked men. A lot. And she wasn't that careful about contraception. Hannah and I have different fathers and apparently there's a younger brother out there, who we've never met.'

'And your father?'

'I never met him.' She moved away. 'And if you don't mind, I'd rather not discuss it any more.'

'Of course not.' He nodded slowly, his eyes gleaming with perception. 'It's no wonder you hung onto your virginity for so long. No wonder that behind that spiky exterior beats the heart of someone who only ever wanted to be a good girl. But you don't have to spend your whole life paying for the perceived sins of your mother, you know, Tamsyn. It won't make the slightest difference if you deny yourself pleasure, just for the sake of it.'

'You mean, now I've actually lost my innocence, I might as well capitalise on it?'

'That's one way of looking at it. If you could stop being so damned stubborn and think about the possibilities open to you, you might be able to see some of the benefits.'

'What kind of *benefits*?'

He gave a slow smile. 'Well, for a start I could teach you how to enjoy your body. I could show you just how sublime sex can be. Wouldn't you like that, Tamsyn? Wouldn't you like to walk away from this marriage knowing how to please a man, and how best *you* like to be pleased?'

Tamsyn shook her head because she hated his logic. For making it sound as if sex was just another new skill to learn—a bit like when she'd studied to be a silver-service waitress. His words reminded her that she was only here for a short while and soon she would be on her own again—back to her nomadic existence. It made sense to tell him no and to stick to her self-imposed celibacy.

So why couldn't she silence the memory of what it

had been like to be naked in his arms…how he'd made her glow and shout with pleasure and then tremble helplessly in his arms? Why not concentrate on how empty she'd felt afterwards, when he'd left her and gone away? 'It seems so…cold-blooded,' she breathed.

'Does it?' he said softly, as he walked towards her.

'Yes,' she whispered.

'On the contrary,' he husked, pulling her roughly into his arms. 'I would describe this as nothing but hot-blooded.'

The first kiss knocked some of the fight out of her and the second had her hungry for more. And when he cupped his trembling hand over her thrusting breast, Tamsyn moaned with pleasure.

Because it felt good. Way too good to resist. She knew she should tell him no. That being physically close again would put her in danger of something she couldn't understand. But how could she refuse something which felt like this? When he was sliding his hand up the filmy skirt of her dress and caressing the shivering skin of her inner thigh?

'Xan,' she moaned, as his finger edged inside her panties and she writhed with pleasure as he found her wet heat.

'You like that,' he observed thickly.

She was too het-up to reply, but maybe she communicated her need to him. Maybe that was why he halted his intimate caress and picked her up, carrying her effortlessly over to the bed. He unzipped her dress and dropped it to the floor, before laying her on top of the petal-strewn cover.

'I see you wore white lingerie for your wedding day,' he observed thickly, tracing a slow finger over the snowy lace edge of her balcony bra. 'How very traditional.'

'It was the only underwear which didn't show beneath my wedding dress,' she said defiantly.

Xan understood a little now of what had made her so defensive, but the thought left his mind the moment he brushed against the taut wetness of her panties, hearing her gasp as he encountered her sweet spot. He slid the zip of his jeans over his aching hardness and pulled off his own clothes before removing her underwear with hands which were inexplicably shaking, something which had never happened to him before. Yet as he climbed onto the bed beside her, he was forced to admit that this *did* feel different—and this time he couldn't blame it on her innocence. Had all the fuss made by his staff about their mock wedding somehow got to him? As if some of their thankful celebration had seeped into his system, kicking his habitual cynicism into touch, making what was happening between him and the little redhead seem especially intense.

Never had a woman seemed so responsive to his touch. She shivered as he reacquainted himself with every inch of her skin, his lips hungrily kissing her neck and breasts and belly as he began to finger her. He played with her until she was writhing and gasping his name, her fingernails clawing frantically at his shoulders. He remembered thinking that she was going to mark him and make him bleed—and that he didn't care.

His gasps became urgent as he entered her and she cried out with each deep thrust, soft thighs wrapped tightly around his back. And nothing had ever felt this good, thought Xan with delirious pleasure. Nothing.

He wanted it to last and last but she was too close, and so was he. He splayed his fingers over her peaking nipples as she began to spasm around him, and his own orgasm hit him like a speed train.

On and on it went, until at last he collapsed against her shoulder with his lips pressed against her damp and tumbled curls. It was a while before he could bring himself to withdraw from her, but just as soon as he did, her tiny fingers curled intimately around him and he could feel himself hardening again beneath her light touch. He slid inside her for a second time and before too long she was bucking wildly beneath him and crying out his name. Soon after his third orgasm, he lay stroking her head and realising that for the next two weeks of his honeymoon, it was just going to be him and Tamsyn.

He stared down at the satisfied slant of her lips. At the lazy flutter of her eyelashes as she gave a sleepy little sigh of contentment. She snuggled deeper into the crook of his arm and Xan felt the automatic stir of overpowering lust and something else. Something he couldn't seem to define....

Maybe it was panic.

CHAPTER TEN

THE MORNING SUN drifted in through the open windows of the bedroom but Tamsyn kept her eyes tightly shut, listening to the even sound of Xan's breathing. She needed to get her thoughts straight before he awoke. She needed to get her mask firmly in place, knowing he would baulk if he ever realised the truth. That their marriage of convenience was about to get a whole lot more complicated.

How the hell had it happened? At what point during this crazy honeymoon, had she started to care for her husband in a way which suddenly seemed unstoppable? She risked turning her head, to see his ruffled black hair lying against the pillow. Was she such a sucker for affection, that she'd fallen for a man just because he clearly enjoyed having sex with her and they spent long hours romping in bed together?

She swallowed. No. It was more than that. Xan could be *kind*, she had discovered. She'd seen that in the way he was with his staff, but he was also kind to her—and interested. In fact, he'd surprised her by wanting to know her views on all kinds of things. Things which nobody had ever bothered asking her about before—like politics and space travel and global warming. And Tamsyn had discovered how flattering it was when a powerful and successful man elicited the opinion of someone who didn't have a formal exam qualification to her name.

Nearly two weeks into her marriage and she had turned from being a reluctant bride to somebody who found joy in pretty much every moment she spent with her husband. But at least Xan didn't have a clue how she was feeling, because concealment was something she excelled at, when she put her mind to it. She'd had a lifetime's practice in emotional subterfuge. She might now want him, but he certainly didn't want her. That had never been part of the deal. No man had ever wanted her, she reminded herself grimly. Not even her own father.

This marriage couldn't last. It was never intended to last. *And the deeper she fell for him, the more painful their split was going to be…*

Dark lashes fluttered open and Tamsyn saw the cobalt gleam from between Xan's shuttered eyes. He gave a lazy stretch and yawned, before pulling her against his warm nakedness and kissing the top of her ruffled curls.

'And what would you like to do today, *sizighos mou*?' His voice deepened as his hand slipped beneath the sheet and he began to massage one erect nipple. 'Since it's the last day of our honeymoon.'

Tamsyn bit her lip, wishing he hadn't reminded her, especially since tomorrow was the day of their post-wedding party and one which his father had now announced he would definitely be attending. She wasn't looking forward to all his friends giving her the once-over and finding her wanting. Her thick skin seemed to have thinned these last few days and suddenly the thought of having to play the unsuitable wife was filling her with dread.

'We could spend the day on the beach,' Xan was saying, stroking the flat of his hand over her belly.

'Beach sounds good,' she agreed.

'Picnic or restaurant lunch?'

She tried to summon up some enthusiasm. 'Picnic, I think.'

'*Relios.*' He gave a slow flicker of a smile and bent his mouth to her nipple. 'My thoughts exactly.'

Reluctantly, she pulled away. 'I'll go and get showered—'

'Hey,' he protested, his hand reaching out to capture her waist. 'What's the hurry?'

Tamsyn's answering smile was tight as she wriggled free, because the last thing she needed was another example of an easy compatibility which meant nothing. 'I need to speak to Rhea about lunch,' she insisted, jumping out of bed before he could distract her again. 'If we're not careful, we'll end up spending the day in bed without actually having our picnic.'

'And would that be such a crime?' he grumbled. 'Isn't that what honeymoons are supposed to be about.'

'Today it would,' she said briskly. 'I need to speak to Elena about flowers for the party and to Rhea about all sorts of boring things, including canapés.'

There was a moment of silence. 'How quickly you have adapted,' he observed silkily, with a note of something she didn't recognise in his voice. 'You are beginning to sound like a real wife, Tamsyn.'

'And we wouldn't want that, would we?' she questioned brightly. 'Don't worry, Xan. I'll have re-adopted my wild-child persona by tomorrow. The shortest dress, the biggest hair and the most make-up. That should do the trick, don't you think? I can't wait to see the reaction of your friends and colleagues.' She forced a smile. 'And now I really *must* go and shower.'

Moodily Xan leaned back against the pillows and watched his wife sashay across the bedroom towards the bathroom, the globes of her buttocks paler than the tanned perfection of her shapely legs. Frustration heated his blood and his erection throbbed uncomfortably between his legs. Why hadn't he overridden her desire to help with the party and encouraged her to give into a far more satisfying kind of desire instead?

He was still engaged in silent contemplation when she returned, dabbing drops of moisture from her dewy body with a towel before slipping on a tiny yellow bikini, which she covered up with a green cotton dress.

His groin ached as he watched her. He had scheduled this honeymoon to give credibility to their whirlwind union, with the party tacked onto the end to indicate a return to normal life. He had planned to use this opportunity to slake himself of his seemingly inexhaustible appetite for his new wife, before she departed from his life for ever with her divorce settlement clutched tightly in her hand.

But his anticipation of all the sex he wanted had been tempered by caution, because he wasn't used to having a woman around full-time. Even during his longer relationships, he rarely stayed with a lover longer than twenty-four hours at a stretch, because by then he'd usually reached his boredom threshold. The thought of fourteen whole days and nights with one person had filled him with panic and he'd imagined he would be climbing the walls by day three. He'd planned to make an urgent visit to his office in Athens on some hastily constructed urgent business if necessary, using the trip as a badly disguised means of escape.

Only it hadn't turned out like that. He hadn't gone near his computer—not once—and the feeling of being trapped simply hadn't materialised. It turned out that Tamsyn liked her own space just as much as he did.

'Of course,' she had informed him carelessly when one day, frustrated at finding her curled up in the garden reading some lurid crime novel, he had enquired rather acidly whether she'd always been *quite* so independent. 'It's the way I was raised.'

Xan frowned. Was it contrary of him to find himself resenting the fact that she seemed intent on racing through the pile of novels she'd brought with her from England? Or excitedly informing him that his infinity pool gave her the ideal opportunity to perfect her breaststroke? And what about the afternoon when he'd fallen asleep beneath a pine tree and she had slipped away. He'd awoken up and gone looking for her and found her in the kitchen with Rhea, who was showing her how to make baklava which Tamsyn seemed to be alternating with colouring in a picture with Gia's young daughter Maria. This scene of domestic bliss should have spooked him but it hadn't, mainly because she had looked up at him with those big green eyes, and smiled and at that moment he had felt completely enslaved by her.

Xan scowled as he pushed away the rumpled sheet and got out of bed. The sooner he got back to work the better, he thought grimly. Work and distance would allow him to put this whole crazy marriage in perspective and to see it for what it really was.

Out on the sun-washed terrace, they breakfasted on fruit and honeyed yoghurt, served with strong black coffee. Afterwards Xan sailed his yacht to a sheltered cove—a favourite place whose inaccessibility always guaranteed privacy. Beneath the deep blue sky they spent the morning swimming and snorkelling in the crystal-clear waters and afterwards drank homemade iced lemonade. But although the food Rhea had stowed away in a cool box was carefully unpacked and looked delicious, he noticed Tamsyn seemed as disinterested in their picnic lunch as he was.

'Not hungry?' he murmured as he lay back on the soft sand.

She sat, ramrod-straight, looking out to sea. 'Not really.'

'Not for food?'

She cleared her throat. 'Something like that,' she agreed reluctantly, as if she resented his perception.

He smiled as a whispered fingertip down the entire length of her spine soon had the tension leaching from her shoulders and the touch of his lips which followed made her give an impatient little wriggle. He brushed his hand against her breasts and saw her lips open with hunger, clamping shut afterwards when he teased her by moving his fingers away from the thrusting nipple. He waited until he sensed complete readiness and then pulled her down next to him.

'Is there anything you want which I can give you?' he drawled lazily.

'Xan,' she said shakily.

'Neh?' he replied, as he stripped the tiny yellow bi-

kini from her body and the sight of her naked in the sunshine made his blood roar. Tearing off his trunks with impatient hands, he parted her thighs and pushed deep inside her and she gasped as her hips lifted up to meet the hard slam of his. Never had she felt so hot or wet or deep and Xan could do nothing to stop the thoughts which flooded into his head as he drove into her. In a couple of days time he would be in his office in Athens, with back-to-back meetings and conference calls. He wouldn't see Tamsyn until he got home in the evening—probably not before eight at the earliest—because he always worked late. Was it that which made this seem so *poignant*? The sense of something ending which somehow increased the intensity, making his climax explode at exactly the same time as hers, which had never happened to them before.

They lay there afterwards, resting in the shade of rocky outcrop and for a moment he thought she was asleep. But no. He heard her sigh as, her eyes concealed by her shades, she stared up at the sky above.

'Was that good?' he questioned, with sleepy satisfaction.

'It's always good.'

'I don't know how you do it.' He gave another yawn. 'But every time I have you, I just want you all over again.'

'It's because you know it's only temporary,' she said lightly.

'Maybe.'

Tamsyn heard the sound of his breathing deepening and a quick glance at his supine form told her he'd fallen asleep. Reluctantly she dragged her gaze away from all the unleashed power of his magnificent body and stared out to sea. Out on the horizon was nothing but a deep slash of dark sapphire water and in front of it, the sugar-white grains of sand. The air was still and warm and fragrant and her body felt utterly satiated by Xan's sublime lovemaking. She wished she could capture that moment and keep it in a bottle.

But she couldn't.

She couldn't hold onto any of this. It was slipping through her fingers just like the fine sand on which she lay. She'd agreed to a three-month marriage but now she could see that her decision to put a time limit on their union might have been too hasty. Even reckless. How could she possibly endure another ten weeks of pretending that her feelings for Xan hadn't changed—when she was putty in his hands after a mere fortnight together?

Behind her dark glasses, Tamsyn blinked away the incipient threat of tears. She'd been told by men in the past that she was cold and frigid. That behind her vibrant exterior was nothing but ice—and she had believed it, because nobody before Xan had ever made her melt. But Xan had. How could she not grow closer to a man when he was inside her and they were staring deep into each other's eyes? When she became unsure where he began and she ended—as if they were both parts of the same body. That was when wishful thinking found an opportunity to creep into her mind and take root there. Started making her long for things which were never going to happen.

Because none of this was real, she reminded herself. They were just playing make-believe. Her Greek husband had embraced the physical, but his emotional barriers remained firmly in place. And so did hers, if she was being honest. Because otherwise, why hadn't she just come out and told him about her dad?

She swallowed. She'd never discussed her father, not even with Hannah. Especially not with Hannah— not after what had happened. Perhaps if she'd fallen in love with someone kind and approachable, she might have opened up her heart to him. But Xan wasn't that man. His lovemaking might be completely fulfilling— but that didn't detract from his hard and critical side.

He'd married her to get himself out of a tight corner.

An unsuitable wild-child bride he just happened to be sexually compatible with.

And the longer she stayed with him, the more vulnerable she made her already damaged heart.

CHAPTER ELEVEN

'So WHAT'S ALL this about?' questioned Xan softly.

Tamsyn didn't immediately look up from the mirror. She was going to need her best smile to get through the next few hours, so maybe she'd better practice composing her face accordingly. Straightening up, she slowly turned to face her husband, stupidly gratified by the instant desire she could read in his eyes. And she wasn't supposed to be feeling *gratified*. She was supposed to be distancing herself from the charismatic Greek billionaire, not revelling in the physical power she could still—unbelievably—wield over him.

'What's what all about?' she murmured absently.

'Don't act like you don't know what I'm talking about, Tamsyn,' he said, treating her to another assessing look. 'I'm just wondering why the sudden dramatic change of image for tonight's party.'

'Could you be a little more specific, Xan? What exactly are your objections?'

Objections? Xan's throat dried to dust. Who said anything about objections? It just wasn't what he'd been expecting, that was all. His wife was wearing a white dress—as befitting a new bride just freshly back from honeymoon—but the outfit was a world away from the flirty mini which had barely covered her bottom on the day they'd wed. This concoction was made from a rich, heavy silk which moulded every curve of her delicious body yet fell decorously to the knee. Her hair had been coiled into an elaborate style, the lustrous curls tamed and gleaming like silken flames, with only a few strands left dangling, drawing attention to the swan-like length of her neck. The strappy silver sandals which gleamed against her bare feet were the only frivolous thing about her tonight, but even they exuded a certain class and style. This was a Tamsyn he'd never seen before. Sophisticated. Elegant— and the very opposite of unsuitable.

'It doesn't look like you,' he observed unevenly. 'This isn't the edgy little redhead I know.'

A flash of colour flared into her cheeks. 'So you don't like it?'

He gave a short laugh. 'Tamsyn, you could wear sackcloth and I'd still want to rip it from your body. I'm just not sure what has prompted this sudden transformation.'

She wound a strand of hair around her forefinger, so that when she let it go, it sprang into a perfect little ringlet which brushed against her neck. He suddenly thought how slim she looked—and how breakable.

'I'm a chameleon,' she said flippantly. 'Didn't you know? I can be whatever people want me to be and tonight I've gone for the sleek and understated look.'

His mouth twitched. 'Any particular reason why?'

She shrugged. 'I've seen the guest list.'

He raised his brows. 'And?'

'And it was exactly as I could have predicted.' She tilted her chin defensively, her eyes momentarily uncertain, as if deciding whether or not to tell him. 'Rich people. Well-connected people. The current darling of the Greek cinema who just happens to be bringing two hulking great bodyguards with her. An international politician or two—including a man they're describing as the frontrunner candidate for the next-but-one US Presidential election.'

'What do you want me to say? I've known Brett since I was at college and to me he's just someone I learnt to play tennis with at Harvard.' He raised his brows. 'I offered to fly your friends over and put them up in a local hotel, but you refused.'

Tamsyn bit her lip. It was true, she *had* refused. Was that because she'd been terrified one of them might see past all the trappings and pick up on the heartache which was building inside her, minute by minute? Or because she was determined to keep her old enemy—pity—at arm's length? She wanted to remember this night as you might remember a particularly beautiful rainbow, or sunset—something amazing but short-lived.

Her sister wasn't coming either, citing a busy royal diary which was planned weeks in advance and didn't allow for last-minute invitations to rushed weddings. But Tamsyn had detected a strong sense of disapproval in Hannah's reply as well as disbelief that she'd actually tied the knot with Xan Constantinides. Tamsyn had wanted to write and tell her she was doing this mainly for her, but her sister suddenly seemed a very long way away.

'Those are the kind of people I associate with, Tamsyn,' continued Xan quietly. 'You knew that.'

'Yes. But it's one thing knowing something and another thing facing them all for the first and probably only time—and that includes meeting your father. I've realised I don't want to turn myself into some sort of spectacle—some caricature of a tart, who people can poke fun at and laugh about behind their back. I've realised I don't want to be *unsuitable*. Not tonight. If I do that it's going to make this evening even more of an ordeal.' She expelled a sigh. 'If you want to know the truth, I'm beginning to wish I'd never agreed to throw the wretched party in the first place.'

He gave an odd kind of laugh. 'Well, just for the record, so do I and if people weren't already on their way from halfway across the globe, I'd consider cancelling it. But we can't. Which means we just have to get through it and make the best of it.' An unwilling kind of admiration sparked in the depths of his dark blue eyes. 'And just for the record, it's a very beautiful dress. You look every inch the suitable bride.'

Trying not to be swayed by his soft praise, Tamsyn smoothed down the silk-satin bodice of the outfit she'd ordered online from a store in Athens and which Elena had smuggled in yesterday. It had given her a ridiculous amount of pleasure to see herself looking like the kind of bride she'd never thought she could be, but in the end—her clothes were irrelevant. All she wanted was for tonight to be over, so she could start thinking about her future.

She watched him walk over to the open windows of their terrace, thinking how much she was going to miss this. And him. She could hear the chink of glasses from out on the lawn as waiters began loading up their trays and in the distance, could see a long line of approaching headlights travelling along the coastal road.

Her eyes ran over Xan's powerful physique, trying to commit it to memory. The snowy white dinner jacket which contrasted vividly with the close-fitting dark trousers. She loved the way those coal-black tendrils of hair brushed against the collar of his shirt, reminding her that he looked as much at home on a sailing boat as he did a boardroom. But as he turned around she quickly wiped her face clear of emotion—eradicating all the yearning, so she was able to meet his cobalt gaze with nothing more telling than a look of cool enquiry.

'Let's go,' he said abruptly.

Xan felt the adrenalin pumping through his body as he took Tamsyn's hand and led her out into the garden, where burning flames lined the paths and fairylights were strung from the trees. The huge swimming pool had been illuminated with floating lights, which gleamed in the turquoise water like surreal water lilies and the front of the house had been floodlit in soft colours of rose and blue. He told himself it was pride in his beautiful home which was making him feel so pumped-up tonight, but it was more than that. He looked at the woman by his side, thinking that Tamsyn had never looked lovelier. The most beautiful woman he had ever seen.

Easily visible in her white gown, he watched men turning to stare at her, just as they had once done at Kulal's palace. Back then he remembered feeling nothing but a destabilising lust but now that had been overridden by a primitive satisfaction that she belonged to *him* and only him. His mouth hardened. But she didn't, did she? Not really. She was his only for a little while longer and he needed to accept that soon she would be free, because that was what the plan had always been.

Free for other men to pursue and to benefit from all that shining sexual promise which he had awoken. A powerful surge of jealousy coursed through him, even though jealousy had never been his thing. He told himself that the feeling would soon pass. That he'd never relied on a woman before and didn't intend to start now. His life had been fine before Tamsyn Wilson had fallen into it like some wayward star, and that state of affairs would resume once they'd split.

Slightly mollified by his own reasoning, he introduced her to a number of guests and she responded with a charm which was contagious. Everyone wanted to talk to her and she instantly hit it off with a European princess, herself a former wild-child, and he could hear the two of them giggling together. Soon she was deep in conversation with a sultan she'd met at her sister's wedding, and several other desert princes moved to join in with the conversation, so that very quickly she was at the centre of a significant power hub. At one point she looked up at him and he raised his glass in mocking salute, as if to silently remind her that her fears of blending in had been groundless. But something in the gesture made her eyes grow dark. He saw her bite her lip and a few moments later she murmured to him that she needed to speak to Elena, and slipped away.

Xan accepted a glass of champagne and looked around. A group of musicians were playing traditional Greek music and out of the corner of his eye, he noticed that Salvatore di Luca had arrived, with the requisite glamorous blonde hanging from his arm like a glittering accessory. But there was still no sign of his father.

He took a sip of his drink. Was the old man worried that Sofia's father would refuse to sell him the island after all—and would that be enough to make him cut Xan from his life for ever? His lips hardened into a humourless smile. What exquisite irony that would be—if an island coveted because of its precious links with his ancestors, should be the cause of alienating his father from his only son.

He looked around again, his eyes scanning the crowded lawn with dissatisfaction as he realised he was looking in vain for his wife. Xan scowled as he handed his half-drunk glass of champagne to a passing waiter, the memory of emerald eyes and fiery curls an image he couldn't seem to shift from his mind.

It was all about sex, he reassured himself heatedly. Nothing but sex.

Tamsyn melted into the shadows, trying to gather her thoughts together. Yes, the party was loads easier than she'd imagined—but it was still stressful, which was why she had sought a moment of quiet refuge at the darkened side of the house, at the top of a gentle sloping incline, which gave a fabulous view of the glittering estate. Carefully smoothing down the rich silk of her dress, she sat down on a bench—tempted to kick off her silver sandals but knowing if she did so, she would be reluctant to put them on again. And tonight there would be no barefoot bride, looking like she'd wandered in from a nearby rock festival.

She sat back against the wooden bench and sighed. It had been strangely gratifying that Xan's friends had seemed genuinely happy to meet her. Was that because she had taken charge of her own destiny, so that for once she actually *felt* as if she fitted in—in a way she'd never done before? Even at Hannah's wedding she'd worn her fancy gowns with a distinct air of resentment—probably because she'd been forced to wear them. But tonight she was revelling in the fact that she looked like a bride her husband could be proud of. She'd felt like a grown up and sophisticated version of the newest member of the Constantinides family. And weren't those thoughts dangerous?

A few times she'd found herself beguiled by the elusive possibility of something which could never happen, not in a million years. Of a life here, with Xan. A proper married life together—with a brood of babies and a golden future. And a shared love? Yes. Oh, yes. That was the ultimate dream. But Xan didn't want that. He'd told her so enough times. He didn't *do* love and he was okay with that. So she needed to be okay with it, too.

A sudden lump constricted her throat as she found herself thinking about her mother. About the paperwork which had been discovered after her death. Her mother had been a foolish dreamer, too—and where had it got her? All those stupid poems she'd written. And the letter addressed to her—the daughter she had abandoned. She mustn't forget that. The letter which Hannah had only shown Tamsyn a long while afterwards, which had told her something it might have been better not to have known. Something which for a long time had made her feel rotten to the core—and still could, if she wasn't careful.

She could see the powerful beam of headlights tracking along the road towards the house and from her secluded vantage point, could sense the excited bustle of the guests as a huge car drew to a halt and a man got out. Even from this distance, from the few photographs she'd seen of him, Tamsyn recognised the distinctive curved features of Andreas, Xan's father. She watched as Xan moved purposefully towards the car, but you didn't need to be a body language expert to notice the coolness between the two men. After a brief and business-like handshake, they began to walk towards the house, making no attempt to join the party.

Tamsyn sat on the bench, filled with indecision. She ought to go and meet him. Hadn't that been part of the deal? Her heart was pounding as she moved through the shadows towards the back of the vast house, away from the main party which was mostly happening poolside. For a moment she stood in silence, until she located the sound of voices which were coming from behind the closed doors of Xan's study. Tamsyn frowned. Xan and presumably Andreas were angrily talking over each other, the volume of their discussion getting louder and louder until she heard someone rasp out a curse. She meant to take a deep breath. To knock politely and walk in, but then she heard her own name and it halted her right in her tracks. Tamsyn froze. She almost wished they were speaking in Greek so she wouldn't understand what they were saying, but Xan had told her that after winning his American scholarship, English had been the language he and his father had conversed in, the older man refusing to be outdone by his fluent son.

'You know what kind of a woman she is?' came the ragged accusation. 'When you rang to tell me you'd married her, I had her investigated and discovered she's a nobody who can't even hold a job down. And she looks like a slut in every photo I've seen of her!'

Tamsyn flinched as she waited for Xan to reply and his next words came as such a shock that she had to put her hand against the wall to steady herself.

'She's no slut,' Xan said. 'She's honest and decent and true. And I will not have you speaking about her that way. Do you understand?'

'And you know her mother was no better than a whore?' continued the older man. 'That she has children by many different men?'

'Yes, I know that,' replied Xan slowly. 'But that isn't Tamsyn. She's never really had a chance, but now she's been given one, she's come into her own. She's uneducated but she's bright. She reads. She plays with Gia's little girl—and that child thinks she's an angel. She's funny. You should meet her. I think you'll be surprised.'

'Oh, I'm not denying she's beautiful.' His father gave an ugly kind of laugh. 'But that's the main reason she's here, isn't it? You turned down the chance to marry a woman like Sofia, for her? I've heard she's hot, but so what? Whores usually are. You get what you pay for.'

There was a loud bang, which sounded like a fist being smashed against a desk and Tamsyn was vaguely aware of Xan's furious response, but by then she had started to run. To run and run until she had left the house and been swallowed up by the dense shadow of a fragrant pine tree.

Her brow felt hot and sticky by the time she came to a halt and it took a long while before she had calmed down enough to be able to think straight. Time for her breathing to slow and her heart to stop feeling as if it were going to burst out of her chest. Something made her tidy up the strands of hair which must have escaped during her run and to extract a slim tube of lipstick from the concealed pocket of her dress, before applying it to her trembling lips with shaky fingers. Her dress was smooth and she needed her features to mimic that smoothness, so that to the other guests it would appear as if nothing had happened.

Because nothing had.

Xan's father had simply told the truth—and he didn't know the half of it. And although Xan had sprung to her defence and her heart had melted slightly at his defence of her—it had still been lacking in emotion. He had still somehow managed to make her sound like piece of rock which had been carved into a rough approximation of a human being.

And suddenly she knew she couldn't endure any more. There was no way she could stay here, pretending to be someone she wasn't. If she did that, then these crazy feelings would keep building and building until she was ready to explode. She needed to walk away with Xan never guessing what had happened. To escape, and quickly—but not tonight. Tonight she would continue to play the role expected of her. The shining and loyal wife, basking in her newly-wed golden glow. The woman lucky enough to have finally snared the elusive Greek billionaire.

She drank a glass of champagne before going back to the illuminated swimming pool to join the other guests, chatting brightly and forcing herself to smile as she accepted congratulations. But her stupid heart turned over with sorrow when Xan reappeared and began to walk towards her.

Did he read something untoward in her expression?

Was that why a frown had creased his brow beneath the delicious tumble of his black hair?

'You okay?' he questioned.

She could tell him, of course. She could say she'd gone into the house to meet his father and heard him calling her a whore. But if she did that, the evening would be ruined—and for what purpose? The fact that Xan's father didn't like her should be regarded as a positive, surely? It meant he would be delighted when his son announced they were splitting up. Maybe their own relationship would even improve as a result. What was it they said? Every cloud has a silver lining.

You can do this, Tamsyn, she told herself fiercely. *You've had a lifetime of pretending everything's okay. Of acting like it doesn't matter when other people judge you, or look down their noses at you.*

'Yes, I'm fine,' she said, then cleared her throat. 'Did I see your father arrive?'

'You did.' An odd expression darkened his face. 'But he couldn't stay.'

'Oh? Was he—?'

'I don't want to talk about my father, Tamsyn,' he interrupted, and suddenly his voice sounded urgent. 'I just want to be alone with you.'

Her heart felt like it wanted to break when she heard the note of hunger she heard in his voice, but she couldn't stop herself from responding to it. 'Xan,' she said, mock-sternly. 'We have guests.'

'I don't care about the guests.' His voice dipped. 'There's only one thing I care about right now.'

His smile was hard and his eyes gleamed with an unspoken message. It reminded her that Xan remained a man who always got what he wanted, and right now he wanted sex. Tamsyn shivered as he traced a finger down her arm, knowing she should refuse to go along with it, especially in view of what his father had said earlier.

You get what you pay for.

But her mind was made up. She wasn't going to ruin the night by dwelling on the negative and besides, she wanted him just as much as he wanted her. Maybe even more. Xan had no idea this was going to be the last time, but she did—and wasn't it crazy not to want to make the most of every precious second with him?

'Then what are we waiting for?' she questioned huskily, as she went into his warm and waiting arms.

CHAPTER TWELVE

'WHAT ARE YOU talking about?' Xan stared at his housekeeper in disbelief. 'What do you mean, she's *gone*?'

But he barely listened to Manalena's distressed explanation as he stormed up to the bedroom because the evidence was there for him to see. He shook his head with disbelief as he pulled open one of the closet doors. Only the most basic of Tamsyn's clothes were missing—all the fancy ones remained. His throat dried as he reached out to touch the white gown she'd worn at their wedding party, which he'd almost torn in his eagerness to remove it from her body last night. Her unread books were no longer in a pile beside the bedside table and that wide-toothed comb thing she used to rake through her unruly curls in the mornings was nowhere to be seen.

He dismissed the housekeeper as he saw a note she must have left lying on the pillow, striding across the room to pick it up and resisting the desire to crush it to a pulp within the palm of his hand. It was short and to the point. Was that deliberate? Was she mocking him for that terse note he'd once left *her* in a faraway desert palace?

Xan,
I've decided to go sooner rather than later and I
didn't want the bore of saying goodbye, I'm sure
you'll understand.
   Below you'll find all my bank details and I
look forward to hearing from your lawyer.
Yours, Tamsyn.

He stared at it, his eyes scanning the words in disbelief, as if there had to be some kind of mistake. But there was no mistake. There it was, in black and white. A stark farewell, which seemed mainly concerned with getting her payment for their short-lived marriage.

His mouth twisted. He'd gone back to the office this morning, strangely reluctant to leave the seductive warmth of his wife's body and the lazy caress of her arms after their surprisingly satisfactory honeymoon. The day had seemed to drag in a way he wasn't used to and several times he'd found himself picking up the phone to ring her, just to say hello, before reminding himself that wasn't his style and putting it down again. He'd told himself it was normal to be physically aching for her, because they'd been having so much amazing sex since the day of their marriage and they'd been together exclusively for fourteen days and nights. Elena had looked startled when he'd suddenly announced he was leaving early and his heart had been beating like a drum as his car had been driven at high speed to the estate, only to discover that his wife had gone. And to discover just how she had spent *her* day...

A bitter taste coated his throat. She must have

been silently planning her get-away. How long had she been plotting that, he wondered? While his own driver had been busy ferrying him around the city, she had persuaded Manalena to call her a cab to take her into Athens, supposedly on a shopping trip—before slipping away to the airport to catch a regular flight to London. Had she been laughing quietly as her lips had locked against his that morning, knowing what a surprise she was about to spring on him? Was that why her hand had slid between his legs to find his hardness—he was always hard for her—and guided him inside her slick, waiting heat for one last, bone-melting time?

He paced over to the window but the bright beauty of the Aegean failed to stir his heart, for his rage and incomprehension were all-consuming. Didn't she owe him the common courtesy of telling him she was breaking their agreement by leaving early, or at least explaining why?

He told himself not to do anything. To give himself time to calm down. But even as he thought it, he found himself lifting his phone and barking out instructions to Elena to have his private jet made ready. He didn't know what he was going to say to his runaway bride, all he knew was that he had to say *something*.

Tamsyn stared at the photograph, as if doing so could help. It was that old trick of voluntarily subjecting herself to pain before anyone else got the chance to do it. As if that could somehow make her immune to it.

Some hope. The photograph was from a gossip column and had obviously been taken at the wedding party. She didn't imagine Xan's friends were the type who sneaked photos at exclusive social events, but there had been a lot of outside caterers there that night and maybe one of them had captured the moment. And, oh, what a moment to have captured.

Beneath a headline which proclaimed *Greek Tycoon Weds at Last!* was a photo of her and Xan. She thought how dreamy she looked and how *happy* she seemed as she stared up into his face. And Xan? Tamsyn sighed. His darkly contoured features gave little away, but maybe it was good to recognise that. To reinforce that she'd done the right thing in running away from his luxury estate, because if she'd stayed around, growing fonder and fonder of him—then her heart would have been truly broken.

Yet didn't it feel a little bit broken now?

From a long way downstairs she heard the doorbell ring, but she didn't move. It wasn't her house—she was just lucky that her friend Ellie from the Bluebird Club had an attic room going free and had told Tamsyn she was welcome to stay there until she'd found her feet again. Funny expression, really. As if someone could lose their own feet. She couldn't imagine going back to waitressing, yet neither could she summon up the enthusiasm to enrol in college to get herself a late-in-the-day education, despite Xan's faith in her. And the craziest thing of all was that, having married just to get her hands on his money, she now found herself reluctant to take any of it. The deliberately cold note she'd left for him had been nothing but bravado—done to ensure that he would ultimately despise her and leave her in peace.

'Tamsyn!'

It was Ellie. With a sigh Tamsyn got up off the single bed, walked across the tiny room and stuck her head outside the door. 'Yep?' she yelled down.

'There's somebody here to see you.'

Tamsyn blinked. Nobody other than Ellie knew she was back, because that was how she wanted it. Time to lick her wounds and recover—even if right now that seemed like an impossibility. She'd told Hannah she was here, in a rushed phone call to the palace in Zahristan when she'd tried her very best—and somehow succeeded—in not sobbing her heart out as she explained that her brief marriage was over. Surely her heavily pregnant sister hadn't impulsively flown over to see her?

'Who is it?' she called back.

'Me,' said a dark, accented voice which carried up the stairs. 'Your husband.'

Tamsyn clutched onto the door handle, trying not to react as she saw a glimpse of the top of Xan's dark head as he walked up the stairs. A lurch of joy and fear made her feel almost dizzy, but most of all she could feel an overwhelming sense of yearning as his broad shoulders came into view. But she wasn't going to let him know that, because one thing she knew was that there could be no going back. She could be strong, yes—she'd spent her life trying to be strong in the face of adversity. Just not strong enough to stay with a man who was never going to care for her.

'Xan,' she croaked, as he drew closer. 'What…what are you doing here?'

'Not now,' he said grimly as he reached the top of the stairs. 'In private.'

'Everything okay?' called Ellie's anxiously from the bottom of the stairs.

'Everything's just fine,' said Xan, in the kind of tone which broached no argument.

Tamsyn felt even more dizzy as he reached the top of the stairs and gestured for her to proceed him into the room, still with that same grim expression on his face. She told herself she didn't have to let him in. After all, it was *her* room, not his—and technically he could even be described as trespassing. She could tell him to leave and only to contact her through her lawyers, but deep down she knew that wasn't an option—and not just because she didn't actually *have* any lawyers. It was more because she wanted to feast her eyes on him one last time. To file away the memory of those cold blue eyes, that hot body, and the sensual mouth which had brought her so much pleasure.

'So, Tamsyn,' he said, once he was inside the miniscule room and completely dominating it, having flicked a dismissive glance at the tiny bed and the view out over an alley which was lined with overflowing dustbins. 'Are you going to explain why you decided to run off without telling me?'

Her heart was beating very fast as she sucked in a deep breath. No, she wasn't. Because she didn't owe him anything. Nothing.

But the defensiveness which had always been second nature to her wasn't coming as easily as usual and she wondered how convincing her nonchalant shrug was. 'We both knew it had to end sometime,' she said carelessly. 'I just made an executive decision to end it early. It was a fake marriage, Xan. It was conceived to get you out of a tight spot and as far as I'm concerned, I've performed my part of the bargain.'

'Why, Tamsyn?' he said simply.

Once again, she shrugged, even though when he said her name like that it made her want to cry. 'I heard… I heard you talking with your father.'

His eyes narrowed in comprehension and then he nodded. 'Did you now? So you will have heard me defending you.'

'Yes, I heard you. Thanks.'

He looked at her. 'And that's it?'

She nodded. 'Yep, that's it. There's nothing more to say. I don't even know why you're here.'

'Because I don't understand. And I need to understand.'

She shook her head so that her unruly curls flew all around her shoulders and impatiently she pushed them away. 'No,' she negated heatedly. 'You don't *need* to understand, Xan. You *want* to understand—and there's a difference. I know you're rich and powerful, but even you have got to realise that you can't always get what you want. So will you please go?'

He shook his head. 'There's something you're not telling me, Tamsyn.'

'And? What if there is? You're not privy to my innermost thoughts—even if we were a real married couple, which we're not! You have no right to expect explanations.'

'I disagree,' he said coolly. 'I think I do, and I'm not going anywhere until you start talking to me. I want the truth, Tamsyn. I think you owe me that, at least.'

Did she? Did she owe him *anything*? For the sexual awakening, or for making her realise that she was as capable of love as anyone else? As she stared into his resolute face, Tamsyn recognised she was in real danger here. She wanted her heart to stop hurting but the only way that was going to happen was if Xan went away and left her alone, and he wasn't showing any sign of doing that. She could see the look of determination on his face and realised he meant it when he'd said he wouldn't be satisfied with anything but the truth.

So should she tell him and witness his disgust when he realised what kind of person he'd really married? Watch his gorgeous face freeze with fastidious horror when he learned the truth about her gene pool? And that might that be the best outcome of all, because then he really *would* say goodbye and she could begin the long process of getting over him. If she pushed him away first—at least he wouldn't be able to turn round and do it to her. She sucked in an unsteady breath. 'You described me as honest and decent and true,' she said quietly. 'But I'm not. At least, I'm not honest.'

'What are you talking about?'

Don't let your voice shake. And, above all, don't cry.

'You only know half the truth. That my mother was a groupie—'

'Yes, yes. That's old news,' he said impatiently.

She shook her head, but her determination not to cry was failing her. She felt her eyes brimming with tears and saw Xan flinch, as if he found such a spectacle distasteful. He probably did. He didn't like emotion. It was messy and he wasn't used to it. Well, neither was she if it came to that, but for once in her life Tamsyn was finding it impossible to hold back the shuddering sob which seemed to erupt from the very bottom of her lungs.

'Well, here's some hot-off-the-press news!' she snarled. 'My father was a rock star. A very famous rock star. His name was Jonny Trafford.'

'Jonny Trafford? Wow.' He frowned. 'But he—'

'I'm not interested in how many albums you had of his. You want to know what happened?' she rushed on, waving her hand impatiently to silence him in her determination to tell him the facts. The unvarnished facts—not the version which everyone knew. It was the only thing she had left of Jonny Trafford—her few brief and bitter memories. 'He had a one-night stand with my mother.' Her voice shook with something like shame. 'According to his official biography, he had similar nights with lots of women. Sometimes with more than one at the same time...'

'Tamsyn—'

'Shut *up*!' she declared as the tears now began to stream down her cheeks and the words came choking out. 'You know my mother had us fostered because we got in the way of her latest love interest? I know. Shocking, isn't it? And after she died Hannah came into possession of her paperwork, including a letter addressed to me which contained the bombshell discovery that Jonny Trafford was my father. But Hannah didn't tell me that. At least, not straight away.'

He narrowed his eyes. 'Why not?'

'She was trying to protect me, just like she'd always done.' Tamsyn stabbed at her wet cheeks with a balled-up fist. 'She thought I'd been through enough hurt and wanted to make sure I wasn't going to endure any more. So she went to see him.' Her voice tailed off but his face was intent as he leaned forward.

'Tell me, Tamsyn.'

She shook her head as she looked at him, knowing this was it. The words tasted sour as she began to speak them but she forced herself to keep looking at the man she had married, no matter how much it hurt. No matter how much disgust he showed when he heard the truth. 'He was a full-blown junkie by then, of course. She said she'd never seen anyone look so pathetic, in his huge mansion with all those great big mirrors and shaggy rugs, and the dusty platinum discs on the walls. But when she told him about me, she said she thought she saw a light in his eyes. He told her straight off he was going to go into rehab, like his manager had been nagging at him to do for years, and he did. And that was when she told me about him.'

'Well, that was good, wasn't it?' Xan questioned.

Tamsyn shrugged. 'Yeah, I suppose so. He wasn't allowed any contact with the outside world for six weeks, not until he was properly clean, but he was allowed to write letters. He wrote to me and said he was looking forward to seeing me and I can remember how excited I felt. I had no real memories of my mother, but here was the chance to connect with my roots at last. I know it sounds stupid but I wanted to see if I had the same nose, or eyes, or if we walked in a similar way. I wanted to feel *connected.*'

'It doesn't sound stupid.' There was a pause and his eyes were very steady as he looked at her. 'What happened?'

'We arranged to meet in a famous London hotel, for tea, but...' She swallowed, then shook her head and it took a couple of moments before she could compose herself enough to continue. 'He couldn't face it—or maybe the lure of heroin was stronger than the thought of meeting his daughter for the first time. I sat in that fancy hotel for ages with barely enough money to pay the inflated price of the pot of tea I'd had to order.

I remember getting lots of pitying looks—probably because of the way I was dressed. Or maybe people thought I'd been stood up. Which I had, I g-guess.' She swallowed again, but now the tears were like hot rivers coursing down her cheeks and the pain in her heart was fierce and intense as she relived a scenario she hadn't allowed herself to think about for years. 'When I came out it was dark and the evening news bulletins were flashing up on TV screens in a nearby department store—and the lead story was that Jonny Trafford had been found dead in a hotel room with a needle hanging out of his arm.'

'Tamsyn—'

'No!' she interrupted, her voice trembling as she fished a tissue out of the back of her jeans and loudly blew her nose. 'Don't say all the things you think you're supposed to say. Because words won't change anything, Xan. I know it was terrible but I've come to terms with the fact that neither my father nor my mother wanted me, and that's why I'm so screwed up. Whichever way you look at it, I'm not the right type of wife for you. My unsuitability runs deeper than you thought and it's far better we split now, rather than later. So just go, will you? Go now and leave me in peace.'

He shook his head. 'But I don't want to go.'

'When will you get it into your thick skull that I don't care what *you* want?' she flared back. 'I'm telling you my wishes and since this is my home, for now at least, you will have to listen to them!'

But Xan didn't move. There was silence for a moment as he glanced over his shoulder to survey the bleak view outside the window and then looked back at her, the woman he had married. He saw the way her lips quivered with belligerence and pride and shame. Her cheeks were wet and streaky and fiery strands of hair were matted with tears. Her expression was defiant but wary as she returned his gaze—like a dog which had spent its life being kicked but had just enough spirit left to fight back. And that was Tamsyn all right. He admired her spirit and always had done.

He hadn't been expecting yet another layer to her tragic life story. He hadn't realised just how deeply she'd been damaged. He'd imagined coming here today and after some token resistance, the two of them having some pretty urgent sex up against the wall, since that bed looked way too small to accommodate two people. Unwilling to let her go just yet, he'd planned to take her back to Greece, thinking that a few months more of his feisty spouse would be enough to get her out of his system.

But now he recognised that he couldn't do that. He couldn't pick her up and put her down, using her like his own sexy little toy. To do that would be to dishonour and disrespect her—and damage her further. Didn't she deserve every bit of his respect after what she'd been through? His heart clenched, knowing that if he wanted this to work—he was going to have to give more than he'd ever given before. He was going to have to have the courage to open up and confront his feelings—just as she had done with him.

'You know that with you, it's like it's never been for me before,' he said softly.

Her emerald eyes clouded with suspicion. 'What are you talking about?'

'I'm talking about you. How different it is with you.

It's been different from the start, Tamsyn—in every way. You're fresh and feisty and original—and more fun than any other woman I've ever known. And we're alike. I see that now. We both grew up rejected by our mothers. We didn't know how to express love because nobody had ever shown us how.' He sucked in a deep and unsteady breath. 'The thing is that I think we could be good together. Not for three months, or a year—but for ever.'

'For ever?' she echoed, as if this was a concept beyond her comprehension.

He nodded. 'It won't always be easy and it won't always be fun. There'll be bad times as well as good, because my married friends tell me that's what life is like. But I think we can be strong for each other and supportive of each other, if the will is there.'

He saw the brief hope which flared in her face before it was banished by that determined little expression of mutiny once more. 'No. It won't work. It can't work,' she husked. 'It'll all end in tears, I know it will. So do yourself a favour, Xan—and get away from me.'

'Sorry.' He shook his head again. 'No I can't do that. You aren't going to sabotage this, Tamsyn—no matter how hard you try. And even if you continue to glare at me and send me away—I'll just keep coming back until you give me the answer that both of us really want. Which is that you will be my wife for real.'

She chewed on her bottom lip as her eyes swam with green tears and it took a full minute before she could form the words. 'You...you really mean it?' she whispered.

He slammed his palm against the left side of his sternum. 'From the bottom of my heart.'

At this she started crying again but this time the tears were different and her mouth was trying to smile instead of wobbling with pain and Xan pulled her into his arms and kissed her with a tenderness he hadn't known he possessed. For a long while they just stood there, locked in each other's arms as their mouths connected in kiss after kiss, and not long after that, Xan made the discovery that the bed was plenty big enough for what he had in mind.

Efficiently, he stripped off all their clothes and it wasn't until he had filled her with his seed and heard her choke out her own cry of fulfilment, that he finally felt as if he was exactly where he needed to be in the world. That everything he'd ever wanted was right here, right now. They lay there, quiet and contented and Xan was stroking Tamsyn's tumbled curls when he tilted her chin to look at him.

'One thing interests me,' he said.

Dreamily, she looked up into his face. 'Mmm?'

'Why didn't you make a claim on Jonny's estate, which presumably you didn't? You could have been a very wealthy woman.'

Tamsyn shook her head. Even Hannah had told her she should try to get something from Jonny Trafford's property portfolio and his back catalogue of songs,, but Tamsyn hadn't wanted to know. 'It all just seemed too sordid,' she said slowly. 'I knew there would be publicity and DNA tests and inevitable opposition to my claim and I couldn't…'

'You couldn't face them?'

'That's right. It wasn't worth it. All the money in the world wouldn't have tempted me to put myself through an ordeal like that.'

He flinched. 'Yet you were willing to marry me for a price.'

She met the question in his eyes and shrugged. 'To be honest, it wasn't for me. I was worried about my sister.'

'Hannah?' He looked at her in bemusement. 'Who's married to one of the wealthiest men on the planet?'

She nodded. 'At the time I wasn't sure if her marriage to the Sheikh was going to last and realised I needed funds to help her if she needed to get away from him. That's why I did it.'

He pulled her closer and his eyes were darkly blue. 'Oh, I love you, Tamsyn Constantinides. I love you because you're strong and brave and loyal. You are the bright fire in my life, my love—and the world would be a very dark and cold place without you.'

Tamsyn swallowed, knowing that there was one thing more which needed to be addressed. 'It doesn't matter what my reasons were, Xan,' she said quietly. 'I still married you for money, didn't I? All your life you've been pursued by women who know how wealthy you are and maybe at heart, you think we're all gold-diggers. I can't blame you for that, Xan. If I were you, I might even think the same!'

He traced his finger thoughtfully over the trembling outline of her mouth. 'Okay. Let's sort this out once and for all. Will you answer me just one question, Tamsyn, with all the honesty you have already demonstrated today?'

She hooded her eyes suspiciously. 'Just one?'

'Just one.' He looked her straight in the eyes. 'If I didn't have a cent in the world, would you be lying with me now, like this?'

It wasn't a fair question because there could be no equivocation about her answer and more stupid tears sprang to Tamsyn's eyes as she nodded. 'Of course I would,' she whispered. 'Because I love you for you, Xan—you and only you. All the other stuff simply doesn't matter.'

His face was serious as he kissed away her tears and only when her cheeks were dry did he turn his attention to her mouth. And the kiss which followed was like no other. It wasn't about sex, or ownership or possession. It was seeking and tender. It spoke of compassion and true intimacy. It spoke of the powerful trust which existed between them now. It spoke of sanctuary and a golden future.

And for the first time in her life, Tamsyn felt safe.

EPILOGUE

'IT'S SO *BEAUTIFUL*,' breathed Tamsyn as the sun sank slowly into the sea, turning the surrounding water into contrasting shades of deep purple and gold.

'I know,' said Xan softly. 'Utterly beautiful.'

Tamsyn looked up to find her husband's gaze fixed not on the magnificent spectacle taking place over the Aegean but on her. 'Xan,' she said, in mock-reprimand. 'I was talking about the view.'

'So was I. But in my mind there's no contest. The sunset on this island is always magnificent—but its blaze is nothing compared to the colour of your hair, *agape mou*.'

Tamsyn gave a shiver of delight as his silken words washed over her. 'If only I'd realised I was marrying a poet.'

'There were a lot of things we didn't know about each other back then.'

Their eyes met. 'But we do now,' she said.

'Yes.'

He walked over to where she stood, on the strip of land not far from the beach. Behind her was the small stone house where their son lay sleeping and in front of her was the endless potential of the night ahead. This was their fourth day on Prassakri, where the bones of Xan's ancestors lay. They'd spent lazy hours walking and talking and teaching their son how to swim. They'd built sandcastles and eaten picnics as they explored the stunning island, where little had changed over the centuries.

But it had been a rollercoaster three years since their wedding.

After initially refusing to sell Xan the island, Sofia's father had eventually agreed on a deal. A deal prompted by the discovery that his daughter was in love with one of his farm labourers, and had been for years—and they needed an injection of cash to start up on their own. Sofia had met Tamsyn and Xan for lunch in Athens and told them everything.

'I knew Papa would never allow me to marry Georgiou because he was so poor,' she'd explained, looking down at her plain gold wedding band with an expression of delight. 'Which was why my long-term engagement to Xan worked so well. It's why I was so happy to go along with it. As a kind of smokescreen, I guess.'

Xan had smiled and so had Tamsyn, glad that no hearts had been broken during the fictitious understanding.

The reconciliation with Xan's father had happened slowly—bolstered by the knowledge that his ancestral island was back under the ownership of the Constantinides family. But the real rapprochement had come after the birth of Tamsyn and Xan's child. Andreas had unexpectedly turned up on the doorstep with a jar of honey—which apparently was a Greek tradition—his eyes filling with tears as he had gazed down at his newborn grandson. These days he came to their house on the Peloponnese peninsula often, enjoying the kind of warm family life he'd never really experienced before.

Tamsyn glanced up at the sky. The sun had almost disappeared and in the darkening indigo sky was the first faint sprinkle of stars.

'I think it's time for us to go to bed, *agape mou*,' observed Xan throatily. 'Don't you?'

Leaning back against his broad chest, Tamsyn nodded. 'Mmm,' she agreed. 'Let's.'

It was still early but they liked to retire early for they enjoyed nothing better than the endless discovery of each other's bodies. The ancient stone steps absorbed the sound of their footsteps as they went upstairs and peeped in on their toddler son who lay contentedly sleeping and sucking his thumb.

'He's worn out,' said Xan approvingly.

'Are you surprised?' She wrinkled her nose. 'He seems a bit young to start playing tennis.'

'That's not what his godfather says.'

'No.' There was a pause while Tamsyn considered the very real chance that her son's godfather would one day be president of the United States of America. She looked down and smiled as she studied the unruly black curls which looked so dark against the sheet. Andreas Alexandros Iohannis. She'd known that another tradition was to call the first born son after his paternal grandfather, but it had been Xan who had suggested including the Greek version of John among his names. At first Tamsyn hadn't known how she felt about that, until a sudden rush of emotion had reminded her that nobody could deny their roots, even if those roots had been allowed to wither, and die. Nobody knew that Jonny Trafford was her father, but echoes of him would live on in her child. She hoped that Andreas inherited some of his undoubted talent, and prayed that they could nurture him with enough love to defeat his demons.

She drew in a deep breath as she stared up at Xan, her heart suddenly beating very fast. 'We won't make the mistakes our own parents did,' she said unsteadily.

'No,' he agreed, his watchful gaze understanding. 'We'll make our own. But we'll try to limit them.'

'Yes,' she agreed as he pulled her into his arms.

'And we'll be honest enough to say if we think either of us is stepping out of line.' He tilted her chin to look directly into her eyes. 'Because we love each other and we're completely honest with each other, Tamsyn—and nothing is ever going to change that. Do you understand?'

Clamping her lips together, she nodded. 'Oh, Xan,' she said eventually, as she touched her fingertips to the roughened shadow at his jaw. 'I must have done something very good in a previous life, to have ended up with you.'

His eyes glinted as he led her from the nursery. 'I like the thought of you being good,' he murmured, as he began to undo the sarong which was knotted around her hips. 'But I like the thought of you being bad much better.'

'Do you really?' she said, tugging eagerly at the zip of his jeans. 'Then I'd better do as my husband desires.'

And she could hear nothing but his growl of contentment as she climbed on top of him in the silver moonlight, and day gave way to night.

* * * * *

COMING SOON!

We really hope you enjoyed reading this book. If you're looking for more romance, be sure to head to the shops when new books are available on

Thursday
9th August

MILLS & BOON

Coming next month

THE HEIR THE PRINCE SECURES
Jennie Lucas

He eyed the baby in the stroller, who looked back at him with dark eyes exactly like his own. He said simply, 'I need you and Esme with me.'

'In London?'

Leaning forward, he whispered, 'Everywhere.'

She felt the warmth of his breath against her skin, and her heartbeat quickened. For so long, Tess would have done anything to hear Stefano speak those words.

But she'd suffered too much shock and grief today. He couldn't tempt her to forget so easily how badly he'd treated her. She pulled away.

'Why would I come with you?'

Stefano's eyes widened. She saw she'd surprised him.

Giving her a crooked grin, he said, 'I can think of a few reasons.'

'If you want to spend time with Esme, I will be happy to arrange that. But if you think I'll give up my family and friends and home—' she lifted her chin '—and come with you to Europe as some kind of paid nanny—'

'No. Not my nanny.' Stefano's thumb lightly traced her tender lower lip. 'I have something else in mind.'

Unwilling desire shot down her body, making her nipples taut as tension coiled low in her belly. Her pride was screaming for her to push him away but it was difficult to hear her pride over the rising pleas of her body.

'I—I won't be your mistress, either,' she stammered, shivering, searching his gaze.

'No.' With a smile that made his dark eyes gleam, Stefano shook his head. 'Not my mistress.'

'Then…then what?' Tess stammered, feeling foolish for even suggesting a handsome billionaire prince like Stefano would want a regular girl like her as his mistress. Her cheeks were hot. 'You don't want me as your nanny, not as your mistress, so—what? You just want me to come to London as someone who watches your baby for free?' Her voice shook. 'Some kind of…p-poor relation?'

'No.' Taking her in his arms, Stefano said quietly, 'Tess. Look at me.'

Although she didn't want to obey, she could not resist. She opened her eyes, and the intensity of his glittering eyes scared her.

'I don't want you to be my mistress, Tess. I don't want you to be my nanny.' His dark eyes burned through her. 'I want you to be my wife.'

Continue reading
THE HEIR THE PRINCE SECURES
Jennie Lucas

Available next month
www.millsandboon.co.uk

LET'S TALK
Romance

For exclusive extracts, competitions
and special offers, find us online: